Dottie

Chattanooga GIRL

DOTTIE COAKLEY

ISBN: 978-1-4834-3021-8 (sc)
ISBN: 978-1-4834-3020-1 (e)

Library of Congress Control Number: 2015906545

Because of the dynamic nature of the Internet, any web addresses or links contained in this book may have changed since publication and may no longer be valid. The views expressed in this work are solely those of the author and do not necessarily reflect the views of the publisher, and the publisher hereby disclaims any responsibility for them.

Any people depicted in stock imagery provided by Thinkstock are models, and such images are being used for illustrative purposes only. Certain stock imagery © Thinkstock.

A percentage of the profits from this book will be donated to groups working on behalf of migrants and farm workers, most especially to those addressing the pesticide issue, and to Alternatives for Battered Women in Rochester, NY.

Lulu Publishing Services rev. date: 04/27/2015

In loving memory

of

Herbert E. Goldsmith

Acknowledgements

My heart is full to overflowing when I think of all the loving support I have received on this journey.

The idea for my book was in its infancy when I timidly joined the Writers' Group at Westhampton Library skillfully led by Kerry Russell. Carol Goodale took over for a while till health issues intervened. It is now presided over by Donna McGullam with a second group, the Writers' Kitchen, on alternate weeks. Janet Nodine was there from the beginning. My thanks to Donna and to Debra Scott of East Hampton for keepin' me one hundred, as Larry Wilmore would say, and to the members of these groups for their input and support.

My wonderful son, John Coakley, his wife, Tessa Addison – thanks for the Prologue idea, Tessa – my daughter, Carrie Coakley, my rock, have along with my brother, John Meyer, and my sister,

Rebecca Robertson, listened to my daily reports on this saga. So have my best friend since the first grade, Carrie Thornbery, and my cherished friends at Glenwood Village. I've benefitted from the valued counsel of Mary Ann Lieberman, Valerie Silverman-Harmon and Jim Kramon. And thanks to my cousins, Tim Mumm, and Deborah Davis, along with my dear aunt, Alice Mariani, for being my cheering section.

I am especially indebted to Mary Ellen Mahland for her superb editing and to Jacqueline Fox for her eagle eye. Thank you is hardly enough for my sister-in-law, Sandi Meyer, computer whiz extraordinaire. Thanks also to John White for "I remember Chattanooga when" and his inspiring pictures.

Ozzie is a very real, loving dog who owns Jacqueline and Daniel Osborne. I met him and them at the New Thought Spiritual Center in Water Mill, NY, a community where I have experienced pure love.

I received encouragement along the way from an amazing adventure led by Susan McArdle and Leslie Handley-White at Joshua's Place in Southampton, NY. But that's my next book.

Most of all, thanks to you the reader for your interest. Any feed-back will be greatly appreciated. And, yes, I acknowledge that the Department of Labor office's location is Newark, New York, not Sodus. I placed it there for personal reasons.

Much love,

Dottie Coakley

He deserves everything he's getting. No regrets. If I leave him here, he's bound to bleed out. That discarded piece of a wooden pallet came in handy. Right when I needed to grab it, it was there. God must be in favor of me getting rid of this piece of shit! A lot of important people will be pleased he's gone. I'm glad he's gone—no more messing up my life! Or putting grand ideas in those farmworkers' heads. One less goddamn do-gooder in this world. I could get used to this feeling. Job well done!

I can think of another do-gooder the world would be better off without. Just need the right time and place. It will come. God may just help me again. I can be patient. She wouldn't be quite so hard to subdue. He put up more of a fight than I expected! But it's worth it. There was never any doubt. No one can stop me. Even God is on my side.

1

At first, Becca Collins felt like a foolish little child, sitting there, tugging at her too-short skirt that kept riding up over her protruding thighs. Why did he keep looking her over from top to bottom? Didn't he know this was the 1970s? Women are not slabs of meat to be weighed and judged by their looks. The interview she worked so hard to set up seemed to be going well. She explained that she was there to negotiate and secure jobs at his factory for her clients—migrants and seasonal farmworkers. Now she was getting angry, and her composure was slipping. She could feel that despised redness creeping up her neck and face. Her friends called it showing her true colors. They always knew when she was angry, no matter how soft her words were.

The employer in question looked across his desk at the nervous young woman making her pitch. He observed that not only was she curvaceous in all the right places but she possessed something he didn't think he had ever seen except on the silver screen—stunning violet eyes, just like his fantasy lover, Elizabeth Taylor. She had a creamy complexion and strawberry-blonde hair that fell in natural-looking waves to her shoulders. He had to have her. That's all there was to it. *This will be easy,* he thought. He held the power here. "So the Department of Labor is under a court order to ensure these farmworkers have access to jobs. Is that it?" he asked in his suave South African accent.

"That's it exactly," Becca replied quickly, trying not to be so aware of the way his long fingers caressed the unlit cigar he held in his raw, sunburned hand. "Do you have entry-level positions open that could accommodate one or more of my workers? They are very motivated and used to hard work. Of course, the Department of Labor will support them in various ways during their transition into your workplace. Acme Transistors would make a wonderful partner for the Department of Labor. We would be pleased to work with you on this."

He got up and walked to the front of his desk, so close she could smell his sour breath. She quickly moved away from him into the solid back of her chair. It made a protesting squeak. Looking straight at her, his eyes narrowing as he closed in on his prey, he made his pitch. "And just what extra incentive could you personally offer me? Convince me to give you these jobs and not some other social worker–type. We could nail down the details over dinner tonight."

Becca immediately stood up. She was completely thrown for a loss. There was no mistaking what he wanted—and no way he was going to get it. Although, for less than one second, she wondered, *What would it hurt to barter for some jobs for my desperate clients?* The thought disappeared as quickly as it came.

The interview was over as far as she was concerned. She moved away from him, almost knocking over her chair. "I have nothing personally to offer you, Mr. Johnson. I'm not available for a dinner meeting. If you want to discuss this further, I'll be more than happy to return to your office for a daytime meeting. You have my card."

Annoyed that she had to stay courteous in order to get some jobs, Becca's inner fighting spirit had to be wrangled in. She couldn't blow what could possibly be a great source of jobs.

"I'm sorry you're not willing to make use of your obvious assets. You have my card if you change your mind," he said.

The interview was over with no jobs to show for it. She made her way out of his office and down the long hallway that led to the building's exit. Becca found her little car in the oversized parking lot. The large number of parking spaces was a painful reminder of the large amount of work available inside the factory. She tossed her briefcase onto the passenger seat, where it found a place amid the flyers and remnants of her hurried lunch. This was just the beginning of the week. She had another group of leads to pursue. Little did she know, job leads would be the least of her troubles during this soon-to-be-memorable week.

2

nother day at the office, Becca thought ruefully as she drove away. In this case, her "office" was her 1976 Dodge Colt, a proud purchase with its first payment from her first New York State paycheck this past August. Becca loved the sporty look of the Colt, its white body topped with a powder-blue cloth roof. Its acceleration left nothing to be desired, which Becca reaffirmed at each stoplight encounter with lesser vehicles. Just now, she had surprised a gorgeous silver Corvette—left him sitting at the light after she carefully but quickly looked both ways and took off. He quickly zipped past her, but that did not squelch her delight at the initial triumph.

She and the Colt were headed back to her stationary office in Sodus, New York, armpit of Wayne County. It was filled with dried-up spaces between deserted buildings and half-starved dogs running around. Just thinking about it always depressed her. Becca's greatest hope and fear was that Brick Wilson, her supervisor, would be making a surprise visit. Becca needed to put some time in on her haphazard record-keeping in order to document the number of migrants and seasonal farmworkers (MSFWs) she had contacted since her last report. She was really bummed not to have new job listings for the farmworkers from her latest effort.

"Damn that skirt, anyway!"

Reminder to self: retire the flashy offender from the work wardrobe choices, meager as they may be. If I didn't hate shopping so much, I might not have this problem, she mused.

Becca let her mind wander back to the delicious dilemma Brick Wilson posed. *Everyone knows you don't mess around with your boss, especially a married one,* she scolded herself. Could the rules be waived if the person in question is bigger than life? What if Robert Redford took a sudden interest in spending one night with her? Would the indoctrination of the church she grew up in allow for the pleasure produced by such a situation?

Nope. Flexibility has never been the church's strong suit. It wasn't hers, either, when it came to married men. Anyway, it was the stuff of delightful daydreaming on her long drives into the country to find the migrant camps entrusted to her care.

Today's rejection triggered the replay of some old stories always ready to take center stage. Becca grew up in the sleepy Southern town of Chattanooga, Tennessee, nestled in the valley between Missionary Ridge and Lookout and Signal Mountains, with the stately Tennessee River winding around Moccasin

Bend. She spent playtime on the side of Missionary Ridge, darting between the cannons left from the Civil War. She also grew up knowing her mother's grandfather had been killed by the Yankees in the War Between the States.

When she was thirteen, her father, who had been diabetic since his teenage years, suffered a heart attack and died. At the grave site following a short service, Becca's mother placed her in a car on its way to Florida. At her mother's request—and until that very moment unbeknown to her—Becca's aunt and uncle had agreed to take Becca into their home. Her younger brother, John, got to stay with their mother and grieve with family and friends.

Months later, Becca asked if she could home. It was agreed that she could, for a price. Her uncle said he would pay her way back to Chattanooga if her mother gave him her father's Indian-head penny and nickel collection. Over the years, her mother told Becca many times it was not a fair trade.

A few years later, she visited her mother and her new husband, Carl, in Illinois. During the courtship, her mother made sure Becca was out of the house—or at least out of the front rooms—so Carl would feel she had only the one young son. After they married, Carl was always friendly to Becca during the few times they were together. On one occasion, Becca and Carl were outside in the driveway, and he introduced her to the next-door neighbors as "my daughter." Becca flushed with pleasure and hurried inside to share it with her mother.

"You did not hear that. He did not say that. You are not his daughter. You are nothing to him. Nothing!" Her mother spat out the words in a voice rarely heard by the outside world, where her saintliness was assumed by one and all. Becca left that visit holding onto the knowledge that Carl did say those beautiful words—no matter what her mother felt about them or about her.

These experiences and more like them stayed with Becca until, even now, at thirty-two years of age, she automatically assumed rejection from other people and automatically felt unwelcome when she walked into a room. Those feelings colored her brief failed marriage to Bill, a New Yorker she had met in Chicago, the nearest big city to the university she attended. Becca and Bill came to the Empire State to visit his parents when he got out of the navy. He got a job at Xerox at a time few companies were hiring. Bill had promised Becca the one state they wouldn't settle in would be New York, so they wouldn't be close to his family. Famous last words.

Surprisingly, Becca had fallen in love with the tree-studded hills and valleys in upstate New York that made her think of her Chattanooga roots. She had grown up believing all of New York was paved in concrete and dotted with skyscrapers. The countryside gently and graciously proved her wrong each day she traveled her territory, the middle third of New York State, which stretched from Lake Ontario to the Pennsylvania border.

Back in the brick-and-cement office, there was no boss in sight, but there was a message to phone him—"very important." Brick was not the dramatic sort, so Becca quickly made the call to Albany headquarters.

"You're getting a helper," Brick told her.

"Do I get to give my input on who this helper is?" she asked.

"No, that's not the way the State does things," he answered. "It's a political appointment. Make the best of it."

"Doesn't sound promising," she muttered, remembering her last disappointing experience of having to work with a teammate.

"You'll charm her. All that Southern sweetness," Brick replied, chuckling as he hung up.

Carolina Jones, the previous Rural Manpower Rep, had patiently explained to Becca on more than one occasion that the two of them were "window dressing." The women weren't really supposed to do outreach to the farmworkers, just on paper fulfill the judge's court order. The farmers were the ones who were the clients of the Department of Labor. All the other Rural Manpower Reps had worked long and hard to establish ties with these same farmers and growers to get their job listings. "The girls" were gumming up the works by offering their workers other options.

A former MSFW herself, Carolina had gone on to bigger and better things. Her charming smile and winning personality had gotten her far, but Becca wondered if her proclivity for missing work, except for payday, would play well in the private sector. She wished her well and would just have to wait and see who her new partner in crime would be.

3

After checking in, Becca headed out again to a run-down section of Lyons, New York, where she had helped a family settle in for the coming winter. Rose and her on-again, off-again boyfriend, Otis, were living in a three-room apartment with a sixteen-year-old son and a four-year-old little girl. Rose was one of Becca's "success" stories. She had placed Rose in a year-round job and helped her find housing.

Otis was an interesting man. He was proud that he had spent a year at a nearby community college and made a point of using correct grammar and pronunciation in his speech. Becca observed that he also seemed to have a quick temper combined with a chip on his shoulder. Could be a dangerous combination.

Lyons was the home base for Golden Smith, charismatic founder of LSW (Learn, Study, Work). LSW made wooden pallets for nearby factories and went out of its way to hire those who needed jobs the most.

Becca was a little concerned by the interest Golden had shown in Rose. He was working on his fourth or fifth wife, she was never sure which. But the current marriage did seem to be sticking this time around. They had produced two little ones to make a tight-knit family

Rose had called Becca at work, asking her to stop over, as she had a problem. *I hope the problem isn't Golden,* Becca was thinking on the pretty drive down 88 and then across 31. A yellow barn was glistening in the sunshine that had arrived after a brief shower. Becca did miss the See Rock City signs that graced many barns on the drive south to Chattanooga.

Golden has been so supportive of all that we do. He's been my backup for the touchiest cases to place. Rose is so warm and appealing. I just hope he has left her alone.

Rose greeted Becca at the door of her tiny but totally neat living quarters. As she entered, Otis pushed past her to get through the narrow doorway. No greetings were exchanged. Becca hoped she hadn't walked into an argument.

"So, how's everything going?" Becca asked Rose as they sat down on a sofa that obviously served as someone's bed, with the sheets and blanket folded up nearby. The fragrant smell of baked corn bread remained in the apartment, possibly leftover from their breakfast time. Becca had to control herself and refrain from asking if there might be a piece left in the kitchen for her to snack on.

"Can I get you some sweet tea?" Rose asked. Becca accepted, both to put Rose at ease and to enjoy a fondly remembered taste from her childhood days in Chattanooga.

"It's Danny, Miz Becca. He's got mixed up with some rough boys, and the police caught them up to no good. He's in jail. And I have to go to court tomorrow, and I can't get there, and I just don't know how to do." The tears came. Becca took her hand, quickly running through her head the list of places where she had planned to go tomorrow. Luckily, the new partner wasn't coming for a couple of weeks, so that wasn't a consideration. Several grower visits could wait till next week.

"I can pick you up and go with you to court tomorrow. I know Golden will understand that you have to miss work. And we'll work through this together."

"Oh, thank you, Miz Becca! I think Otis is heading to Florida right now. I—"

A soft rap on her door interrupted her next thought. "There's a phone call for you out here in the hall, Miz Rose," an elderly neighbor gentleman told her. "Sorry to interrupt, ma'am."

Becca sipped her tea as she waited for the next development. Rose came back bemused. "It was a man, a white man, from Danny's high school, a coach. He says he's coming tomorrow, because he knows Danny is a good person, and he wants to be there for him."

"Did you get his name?"

"Jack something," Rose replied.

"Well, we'll take all the help we can get," Becca declared with a smile. "Now you try to get some rest, and I'll pick you up at 8:15 so we'll be there in plenty of time."

Rose touched Becca's arm, which Becca took to signify a gratitude that was too difficult to put into words. The idea of that saddened Becca.

4

In her car, she decided to go a little farther east and then head north to find a migrant camp rumored to be located deep in the hills of Wolcott. She was going down a road devoid of farmhouses or any other living quarters when she spotted a group of shacks directly ahead. She stopped her car and got out just as a man appeared among the lean-tos and walked toward her. As he got closer, it became apparent that the man had no clothing covering the bottom half of his body. Becca was suddenly aware of the desolation and isolation of the camp she had found. She saw no need to provide outreach to this particular farmworker and quickly made her way back to her Colt, locking the doors before taking off.

Guess that's one statistic I'll have to leave behind! Becca knew she was trying to lighten her mood and regroup. Her hands gripped the steering wheel as she sped away back toward civilization.

She couldn't wait to get home to meditate. Her beloved brother, John, had given her a precious gift when he returned from Vietnam; he paid for her to spend a weekend at a Zen monastery in Rochester to learn transcendental meditation and be given her very own mantra just like George Harrison of the Beatles. Somewhere through all her readings, she had also acquired a phrase that calmed and soothed her in times of stress, anger, guilt, you name it. "Love—That Which created me is What I am." She repeated this as she drove home back to her normal self.

Becca usually made her camp visits at night when the workers were available. She was not anxious to head back out tonight, especially with an early morning tomorrow. Home had never looked so welcoming. Becca had gotten very lucky to find and rent the little cottage on the lake, deep in the apple orchards of Chuck and Mary Browning, growers whom Becca respected. The housing they provided for their workers was quite decent, and they were agreeable to Becca's passing out the Department of Labor's flyers touting the available services.

Her orange-and-white tabby-cat, Rusty Nail, greeted her lovingly. The white stucco cottage felt roomy on the inside, not only a living room on the first floor but also a small dining room. The white walls enhanced the feeling of roominess, and the glassed-in porch facing the lake created even more expansiveness. The soft blue-gray rug seemed to bring the lake inside. There were two bedrooms and a bath on the top floor with views that allowed her to catch sight of the water spouts that danced across the lake on occasion. The kitchen was just right for someone of her limited culinary talent. Tonight, a can of tuna enhanced by a hard-boiled egg and a little mayo would make her life complete. Rusty Nail seemed to feel the same way.

5

The next morning came too soon. For a moment, Becca couldn't figure out why the alarm clock was doing its thing at the ungodly hour of 6:30 a.m. Then she remembered what the morning held for her and Rose and Danny. She debated which outfit to fall into after a quick shower. Her red blazer over a white turtleneck and black slacks felt like a power outfit perfect for today's court appearance.

She picked up Rose right on time. The four-year-old, Nettie Mae, had already hopped on the ancient school bus that would take her and thirty other little ones to their Head Start location at the local Episcopal church.

Rose was a pleasingly plump woman with soft brown eyes, warm tawny skin, and a gentle manner. For court, she had chosen a simple blue dress with a gray wool cardigan to protect against the vagaries of a September day.

"You look very nice," Becca greeted her. "Were you able to contact the public defender's office as I suggested?"

"Someone will be there today, they said," Rose answered. "I just don't know how I'll find money to pay them for their trouble."

"I don't think you have to pay them anything; they get paid by the State of New York to help people who can't afford private attorneys. You pay taxes on what you earn at LSW, and that helps the State to pay them. So you are doing your part to pay them."

"You make everything sound so much better, Miz Becca. And I want to give you some gas money for today's trip and your time."

"The same thing goes for me and my time and my gas. The State, to whom you paid taxes, pays my salary for my time and even pays me thirteen cents a mile for all our travels. Isn't that great?"

"Now that's really something," Rose declared.

Soon they were pulling into the parking lot on Main Street in Lyons. Becca was happy with her blazer choice, as many people in suits were hustling into the courthouse. She noticed one man in a sweater and slacks who stood out in all the busyness. He was attractive without being what she would term ruggedly handsome. He was in his early forties, she guessed. He had sandy-brown hair and green eyes that held hers until she blushed when she realized she had been caught staring at him. He smiled and then headed toward her and Rose.

"Are you Danny's mother?" he asked as he approached them. "You have the same smile." The warmth the man exuded was almost palpable. Becca felt a strong urge to reach out and touch him, if just for a moment. She pulled herself back to the conversation going on around her.

"Oh, thank you, sir. Yes, I am Danny's mother. Are you from the school?"

"I'm Coach Hightower. Please call me Jack. I wasn't sure if there would be anyone here with you. I see you are well taken care of."

"Coach Hightower, this be my friend Becca Collins," Rose said formally.

"A pleasure. How do you two know each other, if I may ask?"

"I represent New York State's Department of Labor," Becca stammered, wishing she could sound more relaxed. "I'm lucky enough to have met Rose because of my job."

"Which is …"

"Letting farmworkers know about the services offered by the Department of Labor and, in some cases, helping them to find yearlong work if they want it."

"Do you do job development? I may need to increase my staff down the line."

"Oh, please let me give you my card. I would love to speak with you about that possibility."

"Fine. Here's my card. Give me a call, and we'll set something up. Now let's see about Danny."

They found seats at the same time that the judge entered the courtroom. Becca was thrilled with their exchange in more ways than one. Sports had always provided her with great pleasure, from her grammar school days of keeping batting averages for her schoolmates to watching the professionals on television. The Buffalo Bills were her favorite football team. She had never had the chance to talk to a real coach before.

The judge looked their way and nodded to Coach Hightower. "Who are you here for today, Coach?" the judge asked.

"Danny Washington, Your Honor."

"Will you have a hand in seeing that he stays out of trouble from now on?"

"He's one of my boys—first-string running back on this year's team in Riverside," the coach answered.

"Good to know."

"How's Harry doing, Your Honor?"

"Graduated summa cum laude from Harvard Law School last spring. He'll be glad I saw you."

"Please give him my best," the coach replied.

Then the clerk started calling cases. A harried public defender rushed in, his arms full of file folders with documents sticking out in all directions. Becca had been hoping for someone with a more professional air about him or her, but in only a few moments, Danny was remanded over to his mother's care with a date set for his next court appearance.

The coach clapped Danny on his shoulder and told him to be sure to be on time for practice that afternoon. No excuses. His leaving was a letdown for Becca, a surprise she was reluctant to fess up to. She had his card securely tucked in her safest place, the middle slot in her billfold. She very much looked forward to their next encounter.

6

On the way back from the courthouse, Rose started explaining to Becca why she had decided to stay in New York year round.

"My fambly's been coming north to work ever since I can remember. But back in the day, my grandmother's brother just disappeared. Poof. His best friend tole us what happened when he got back home. Petey was riding on the back of a truck when it stopped all of a sudden. Then the fellow driving backed up, and Petey was dead. Runned over. But they didn't let us know or have the body. It just disappeared. No one called the sheriff or nothin'. Poof and Petey was gone. I don't want my children in this kind of life that can just make them disappear!"

"That is such a sad story—I'm so very sorry." Becca reached over to grasp Rose's hand for a moment. "This accident happened in New York?"

"Yes, out on Long Island, on the North Fork. We quit going in that direction after we lost Petey. We tried a season in Virginia in the tobacco fields, but Danny got so sick there. We had to take him to the emergency room at the hospital—he was throwing up so, and his head hurt bad. The white doctor there was mad at me. Said he had a poisoning from them long days in the field—no place for a child!"

"Aw, Maw, it wasn't all that bad." From the backseat came a voice trying to be lower than it was.

"How bad was it, Danny?" Becca asked him.

Danny, slouched down in the backseat of Becca's Colt, his scrawny six-foot frame cramped in the tight space between front and backseats, replied, "I guess it was pretty bad—all the puking and dizziness and headaches. And I'll never get ahead of the thirst I had with that blazing hot sun beating down on me."

"Didn't they give you breaks to get a drink of water or anything?"

"There was no water allowed except for maybe one ten-minute water break on a good day. But it didn't suck nearly as much as coming home and finding Ma beaten up by that shithead boyfriend of hers, her face all mashed in. Remember, Ma? You were so sad. So defeated like. I was too little then to take him on, but, boy, I wanted to! I think he's afraid of me now. I've been working out with Coach's help."

"Danny, that's a long time ago. Enough on that. So we got back with the New York crew," Rose continued. "And then you helped me get out from under the farmwork altogether. Danny has had his strength come back and even made the football team now that we can stay in one place. We thank you so kindly!"

"So you are creating a better, more secure life for Danny and Nettie Mae," Becca stated, squeezing Rose's hand again as they pulled up to her apartment house.

"I'm trying, and you are a help."

"Thank you so much. You and the children make my job a pleasure! Does Danny need a ride from here to school?"

"No, ma'am. I'll get a sandwich down him, and then he'll make his way over there. Thank you very much! From all of us."

"Yes, ma'am," Danny agreed as he exited the car.

"Take care, Rose and Danny."

7

Becca made her way back up Route 88 to a grower she had been trying to catch at home. She needed his permission to go on his land and talk to "his" workers. Mr. Jackson was just getting into his well-worn truck when Becca pulled into his driveway. "You can ride with me, and we can talk on the way," he offered. Becca willingly got in the 1970 Ford pickup, a decision she would later regret. Mr. Jackson was not in a happy mood.

"Are you aware of the percentage of jobs—like yours!— that are in the service sector that don't make anything or do anything valuable or concrete?"

Becca knew that supporting Rose and Danny was valuable work … maybe not so concrete. She actually hadn't thought about jobs in such terms before.

As Mr. Jackson continued his tirade, Becca felt more than a little trapped in his truck and was becoming concerned as his anger grew. Yet, as they pulled back up at the farmhouse after having checked his fencing, Mr. Jackson surprisingly gave Becca permission to visit his workers at their camp.

"Be careful of the crew boss, though. Neither of the murder charges was proven, so I've kept him on; he runs a tight ship," he said in a parting shot.

On the road again, Becca could see the traditional-looking high school directly ahead and was suddenly tempted to pull in and try her luck at connecting with the coach. It wasn't very professional to simply show up without calling first for an appointment; however, Becca felt drawn to the place and, of course, to him, and decided to risk it.

She parked her cherished Colt and made her way to the part of the school housing the athletics department. As Becca approached the coach's office, she could hear what sounded like protests of "Fixed! Fixed!" coming from handfuls of high school boys jumping up and down outside the large glass partition. Inside, Coach Hightower was writing his name on the blackboard under the title, "Most Handsome Member of the Riverside Football Team of 1976." The garbage can held what looked like a couple of dozen ballots. Becca would have loved the chance to audit them.

She made her way through the excited football players and knocked on the door. The warmth she had experienced in the courtroom seemed magnified when it was just the two of them, not counting the onlookers outside the office.

"Are congratulations in order?" she asked as she entered his office.

"They certainly are," he answered. "And it's the fifth year in a row—always a happy surprise!"

"I can just imagine," Becca replied dryly. "Coach, as you probably remember, we met earlier today in court when we were there for Danny Washington."

"Of course I remember," he stated emphatically. "Come sit down and tell me more about what you are doing."

She positioned herself in the chair he indicated, which was very close to his desk chair. In her nervousness, Becca dropped the pamphlet she was about to hand to him. As she leaned over to retrieve it, her soft cheek brushed his muscular thigh. A wave of heat pulsed through her body, and she could feel her face flush, but he immediately put her back at ease with a deprecating comment about his "fan club" outside the office.

Half an hour later, Becca felt entirely listened to, understood, appreciated, and supported. Plus, she had a job slot for the farmworker who would be willing to face a New York winter. Jack had explained that he had an unofficial "staff" made up of the shyest misfits—not his term—in the high school. But he could still use an official assistant with his duties as athletic director.

What also came up in their conversation was that the coach was a widower with a son and a daughter. The son, Michael, was a freshman at Cornell on a full football scholarship.

Marcie, a high school junior, had strong leanings toward being a veterinarian as her dream job.

Becca could tell how important Jack's family was to him as he lovingly described them to her. She felt the void in her life as a single woman with no deep attachments to show for her thirty-two years on the planet. There had been some close calls, but nothing stuck—so far.

Her brief failed marriage to Bill had transplanted her from the southern city of Chattanooga, Tennessee, to upstate New York where the tree-covered hills were surprisingly familiar to Becca—a most happy surprise. She had come to love the beauty and earthiness of her new home, even if she hadn't exactly chosen it for herself in the first place. And here was a lovely man showing some interest in her—she hoped.

Back to her cottage to tell Rusty Nail all about the coach.

8

The rain was coming down in sheets. Becca fought the urge to burrow deeper into her blankets. She knew she would possibly find farmworkers at their camps on this dreary day even if it were a Saturday. Becca threw on some jeans and a warm sweatshirt, fed the incessantly demanding cat, and grabbed a bowl of cereal, slicing up half a banana on top for good measure.

On Route 88, she kept trying to see through the downpour to locate the camp that was said to be just below the roadway. On spotting something that could be a camp, she maneuvered her Colt off to the side of the road. She stumbled down the hill, trying to keep her handouts sheltered from all the rain coming her way. The dark skies added to her feeling of being cut off from the rest of the world. The raindrops that had seemed comforting on her roof at home now seemed threatening and ominous. Becca was so hoping that the notorious crew boss, accused of two murders but not convicted or jailed for either of them, would be in town on an errand or anywhere other than the lean-tos ahead of her.

She quickly entered the shack after knocking loudly, and silence fell on the group of men gathered there, some lying on cots, others simply standing around. Becca asked for the crew boss by name, Mr. Bolton, and a very large, rough-hewn man headed straight for her, stopping only a few inches away from her.

He brusquely said, "Who's asking?"

Becca started explaining the Department of Labor's outreach program under Judge Richey's Court Order when the man cut off her spiel.

"You have no right to be here on private property talking nonsense to my people!"

"But I do have a right. I have permission from Mr. Jackson to be here, and this is his property." Becca hoped she could keep her voice steady, as the rest of her person was dying to get the hell out of there.

"I don't believe you. Leave. Now."

"If I may use that phone on the wall, I'll call Mr. Jackson, and he can tell you that what I'm saying is true."

"I still don't believe you. I dare you to call him." Intense hatred and impending violence dripped from his words.

Becca could feel the eyes of everyone in the room. She wondered if anyone there would take her side should Mr. Bolton get physical. For some unknown reason, which she would later call into question, she felt she must make this call and not retreat. These workers were entitled to this information under the law. This was her job. Becca was also painfully aware that no one else in Wayne County knew of her whereabouts at that moment in time. Why hadn't this visit happened after she got her new partner? She had to remember to keep calling into the office with at least the approximate times and locations of her field visits.

She headed for the phone hanging on the wall while fumbling through her papers looking for Mr. Jackson's number. The crew boss followed her across the long room and stood an arm's length away. He towered over her as she made the call, his anger coming toward her in waves.

Mr. Jackson answered on the third ring. Becca shakily told him that his crew boss needed confirmation that she was there with his full knowledge and permission. Then she turned the phone over to the objecting man. She couldn't make out what Mr. Jackson said, but it was short and did the trick.

"Give out your papers, and get the hell out of my place!"

She proceeded to do so as quickly as possible. Not surprisingly, no one expressed any interest in the services that were in direct competition with that of their fearsome crew boss.

She had done her job. Becca scrambled up the muddy hill and welcomed the feel of water on her skin and the sight of her Colt. She surveyed her surroundings to make sure she hadn't been followed. She locked the car doors and put the car in gear for her getaway.

9

Becca's heart was so heavy she thought it might break as she trudged up the short driveway to the beat-up trailer that housed the Hernandez family. She was bringing them a bag of food—some rice, beans, bread, peanut butter, cereal, soup, and Oreos for the kids. The last time she visited, she had loved the delight that danced in the brown eyes of Maria and her little brother, Jesus, when they spotted the sugary treats.

The rusted-out trailer was fronted by someone's past attempt at a flower garden. What remained at this point were only a few stalks curled into themselves for protection and comfort. The middle step leading up to the front door was caved in and dangerous, Becca thought, especially for a pregnant woman to manage.

Their family was missing one of its money earners. Mrs. Hernandez had worked picking apples until the very last moment of her pregnancy, staying off the ladders and retrieving the apples from the ground. There were complications, and the precious baby was stillborn, grossly deformed and misshapen.

Becca felt deep in her gut that all the pesticides in the orchards were a primary cause for this loss of life, not to mention the lack of medical care given the mother. It impressed on Becca the urgency to get the word to these families about the free clinic that had recently opened up in Wayne County.

Even though the baby would have been another mouth to feed, this loving family was devastated by their loss. The darkened house radiated sadness as Becca approached.

While she was knocking on the door, Becca pulled together her few words of Spanish. Last week, she had signed up for Beginning Spanish at the local community college. Becca observed that there were an increasing number of Spanish-speaking migrants entering the work stream.

Mr. Hernandez, the grieving father, opened the door only a crack. Becca offered the bag of groceries with a weak "Lo siento por su problem con el niño … el bebé" in broken Spanish. He accepted the bag and the condolence with a quick, "Gracias, señorita." On this occasion, he didn't indicate that she could enter the home.

So Becca walked away, troubled by what she was not witness to. She promised herself she would find a Spanish translation of the free clinic's services and get it to the Hernandezes. She knew she would have to check back with the social worker who also worked with this family and confer with her on what—if anything—could be done to recompense them in some way for their tragic loss.

10

O n this particular weekend, there was a conference of the Rural Manpower Reps in Syracuse, New York. Becca had planned to stay overnight instead of making the trip back and forth, as it was the State's treat. She figured the cost of the hotel wasn't that much more than the amount the mileage expense would have come to.

At the end of a long day of meetings, Brick invited her to come with him and several other men out to dinner. That was enjoyable enough, if a tad awkward, when Brick and his supervisor, Cliff, invited her to go to a club with them. Becca was always aware of being "the female," so she decided she would try to be "one of the boys." Mistake.

The club the men chose was a strip joint on the south side of Syracuse. When they got there, Becca's thrill of the night came when Brick handed her his drink in a proprietary way that made her insides do a little dance of happiness.

However, the show itself was a big letdown. The women were not at all attractive by anyone's standards, male or female. Becca felt dirty and more than a little disappointed in herself for having participated in the night out with the "boys." So much for blending in.

It crossed her mind that Coach Hightower, whom she'd known all of two weeks, would not have disrespected her this way by inviting her to such a seamy place. It made her feel good to have him as a touchstone, simply to know he was out there and now a part of her world. He had carefully asked whether she would have any interest in a cup of coffee sometime. Her response was immediate and positive. She hoped he wasn't wasting a call this weekend while she was in Syracuse. But she would welcome a blinking red light on her answering machine when she got home.

It was there! First was a call from her brother, John. She would call him back right away, as soon as she checked out call number two.

"Becca, this is Coach Hightower. Jack. Just calling to say hello and to see if we can set something up. If you are interested and have time, give me a call at 315-555-2430. Thanks, Becca."

Perfection! It was four in the afternoon, and he had left the message at one that day. Good connection. She would feed Rusty Nail and then give the coach a call. And call John back.

An hour later, after a very warm, funny, and relaxed exchange with Jack, Becca had a date to look forward to later that evening. She was amazed at how easily the conversation had flowed and the delight she had found in their give-and-take. "Tonight awaits," she sang to herself and to Rusty Nail, hopeful that she could find the same ease with this man when they were face-to-face.

11

That night, she chose her gray wool slacks and a soft white angora sweater. She felt very feminine as she put on her dangly pearl-drop earrings. Carrie, her best friend since the first grade, called this sweater the "Don't you just wish you could fuck me!" sweater—versus the less subtle "Fuck me!" sweaters out on the market.

They had dinner at the elegant Cinelli's right on the shore of Lake Ontario. Becca couldn't remember a night when she had laughed so much or felt so at ease. Several hours later, Jack walked Becca to her door. She invited him in, and he said, "Next time." That reassuring prospect made her very happy.

Then he said, "May I kiss you good night?" That kiss changed everything in Becca's little world. All of a sudden, the world was a friendlier place with all sorts of possibilities just waiting to be discovered. She kept saying to herself and to Rusty Nail, "Funny and sexy—it doesn't get any better than this!" Becca slept well that night after thinking that she wouldn't be able to sleep a wink.

12

The week passed quickly with several phone calls from Jack that Becca treasured.

One camp visit was memorable. When she approached the men that Tuesday night, one of the farmworkers became verbally abusive. Another immediately walked her to the door. Outside, he took out his wallet and showed Becca the picture of a lovely home. It was his Florida residence, a simple ranch house with a vegetable garden out front. He told her that he made enough doing the farm labor to support a nice lifestyle in the wintertime. "That is why some men get offended at you coming in here offering forty-hour-a-week jobs in the snow and cold at $2.30 an hour."

Becca thanked him for his concern for her safety and for his educating her. She felt dismayed that she had been so blind to the other side of the migrants' lives, at least for some fortunate few of them.

Becca knew Jack was tied up Friday night with an important football game. When another school had closed, their rival had acquired some imposing players who dwarfed his guys. Becca decided to go to the game on her own and see Jack in action.

The first half was just as sad as Jack had had a feeling it could be—sadder, even. The other team scored at will, and the score at halftime was 20–0 with Jack's team on the losing end. Second half, Jack's team marched down the field and scored a touchdown. 20–7. Becca jumped up and down, so glad they weren't without a score. End of the third quarter, the defensive end made an interception and took it all the way in. 20–13. The kick for the extra point hit the uprights and then tumbled back in to bring it up to 20–14. They were making a game of it! Fourth quarter with time running out, the quarterback completed a pass to the running back wide open in the end zone. 20–20. "Was that Danny Washington?" she asked the lady sitting beside her.

"Yes, he's in my son's classes," the excited lady replied.

Becca quickly scanned the crowd for Rose. She couldn't pick her out but thought she spotted Otis, Rose's boyfriend, sitting by himself at the top of the bleachers her left. She could see Jack pacing up and down the sideline. She could feel his tension even from this distance. Becca was holding her breath as the team lined up for the extra point kick in the final seconds. Becca grabbed the arm of her new best friend and held on. Instead of the kick, Jack's team ran a play that netted them two points and won them the game. 22–20! The crowd went berserk! Yet, Becca and many others around her were completely puzzled as to why Jack took the chance on the two-point conversion.

Becca tried to get down to where Jack was. He was being pummeled by many happy adults and kids. He saw her and made his way over. "I have to go back on the bus with the kids and then wait to be sure everyone goes home from the school. Do you have any interest in meeting me in an hour or so at Cinelli's for a drink to celebrate?"

"I'd love it!" Becca replied. She quickly moved away to allow the many well-wishers to get a chance at telling him what an amazing game it had been.

An hour and ten minutes later, Becca watched as Jack struggled to cross the room to the table where she waited patiently. He seemed to know everyone in the room—or they each thought they knew him. She felt a quiet happiness to be sharing this special and triumphant occasion with Jack.

After their drinks arrived, Becca couldn't wait to ask him about what was most perplexing to her about the game. "Whatever made you call the two-point play when you only needed one point to win?"

"My kicker came to me, and he was shaking all over. I couldn't put that young man in such a pressure-filled situation, as that final kick with the whole game riding on it. He simply couldn't handle it. A game is just a game, but this was a good kid who didn't need all that pressure. And it took a lot of courage for him to come to me and reveal how scared he was."

I could so easily love this man! Becca told herself. His concern for his kids stood out as his overriding principle—not the fierce desire to win she had earlier observed.

"And what, if anything, made the difference between the first and second halves? It was like watching two different games, two different teams."

"I was so disgusted after that first half! I told the boys to gather up their gear and get on the damn bus—we were going home."

"You didn't!"

"Did too. And once we were on the bus, I tore into them. You wouldn't know it, but I actually have a bit of a temper. I told them in all my years of coaching, I'd never been so ashamed of a performance. 'Let's just give up and go home.' They started yelling, 'No! No!' and by the end of my speech, they were ready to head out the back of the bus if necessary to get back on that field. It's a good thing we couldn't find the bus driver when we first got on. And the rest is history."

Becca was thrilled to be this close to the inside of a football game, not to mention drawing closer to this remarkable man and getting a glimpse of how his brain worked. She was very much looking forward to the rest of the evening when the waiter approached them.

"Coach Hightower, there's a call for you at the front desk."

Jack excused himself and returned a few minutes later. "I'm so sorry! I'm needed at home to straighten something out. Could we continue this at a later date? I'll call you tomorrow, and we'll make plans for a night out all to ourselves, just us."

"All right," said Becca, trying to hide her disappointment. "I'll look forward to your call."

Jack placed some bills on the table and gave her a quick kiss on the cheek. Even that small gesture made her insides do another of its little dances and gave her happy thoughts all the way home. *No red flushes intruded on our evening together. I'm at ease with this man.*

13

The next day was uneventful while she waited for Jack's call. Becca had the usual picking up to do around the little cottage. There was a book she wanted to get lost in, *Sleeping Murder* by Agatha Christie. It was Miss Marple's last case, so it might be Agatha Christie's last book. She would have to wait and see.

Jack called at last. "I apologize that my weekends are so full. Would it be possible for you to fit a lunch into the middle of a workday? Someplace a little closer to my school, like Friendly's? I know this is asking for a lot of maneuvering on your part."

"Sure I can," Becca replied. "I make my own hours, especially since, like you, I work many evenings. Wednesday would be perfect for me. Can I swing by the school and pick you up?"

"That would be very nice of you. I'll be looking forward to seeing you again. I'll touch base with you before Wednesday. Good-bye for now." Jack ended their conversation.

Becca hung up quite happy with their plan and also happy at the thought of a phone call in-between. "Life is good!" she told Rusty Nail as she got back to her book and he settled in beside her.

14

Tuesday night, Becca had responded to the urgency in Golden's voice as he requested that she meet him to discuss a private matter regarding Rose. She had met after hours with Golden twice before, which was not that unusual in their busy lives. However, the factory did feel especially empty at this eight o'clock hour.

Becca made her way to Golden's office down the dimly lit hallway. His office door was ajar, but no sounds of its occupant reached Becca's ear. She knocked sharply, not wanting to barge in unannounced. No reply was forthcoming. Becca pushed the door open farther. She was horrified to see a man's leg angled out from behind the large oak desk Golden treasured. She realized she was holding her breath. She froze just inside the doorway.

He must be hurt. I have to go to him, she told herself. *I must get help!*

"Is anyone else here?" she called out as she made herself move toward the inert body, terrified by its stillness. She approached the corner of the desk, and her worst fears were realized. It was Golden, beaten so badly she doubted that he was alive. Becca grabbed the phone on the desk and shakily called 911.

"We need an ambulance and the police—quickly!—to the LSW factory on Mill Road. Please hurry! Please!" The 911 operator tried to keep her on the line. Becca was so scared—all she wanted to do was leave the brutal scene and be back in her cottage curled up with Rusty Nail.

Then she thought of the coach. She had memorized his number because it was so very important to her. It gave her courage simply to entertain the possibility that he would come to her and help her get through this hellish mess. Thank God the phone was still working.

Suddenly, she heard or sensed a movement just outside Golden's office. Should she call for help again or keep silent? Her heart pounded hard enough to give her away.

Then she heard the welcome voice of Joe, the elderly night watchman. "Is everything all right in there, Mr. Golden?" came through the door.

"No, Joe, please come in. It's Becca Collins. Mr. Golden is here, but he's been hurt. I've called for an ambulance and the police," she continued as Joe hustled in. "We probably shouldn't try to move him or touch anything."

"Dear Lord, Miss Becca, I think the poor man is gone! I just knew those folks would do him in someday—just didn't think it would be today!"

"What folks, Joe?" Becca asked anxiously.

"Them growers didn't like what we was doing here at LSW the least little bit! And what will happen to us if Golden is gone? He didn't deserve this, not at all. No one does!"

Becca had been applying pressure to what looked like the deepest wound with her half slip that she had quickly stepped out of before Joe's arrival, but the amount of blood in pools around him made her feel her efforts were futile. She could detect no motion in his chest to indicate breathing. The metallic stench from the blood was making her ill.

Finally, they heard sirens approaching. "Joe, please go to the entrance and guide them to this office," Becca directed. He hurried out as the sirens grew louder and clearer and then stopped abruptly.

15

Soon, the room seemed full to bursting with the various medical personnel from the ambulance and the necessary police officers. The person who seemed to be in charge strode over to Becca.

"Are you the one who made the call to 911?"

Becca nodded mutely.

"Did you find the body?"

She nodded again.

"Do you know who it is? Have you changed its position? Would you like to sit down?" The last question came as Becca's knees suddenly gave way, and she fell forward into the detective's personal space. He got one arm under hers and led her out into the hallway. They found an empty, smaller office next door.

"To answer your questions, I am the one who called this in. The body is Golden Smith, owner and CEO of LSW, the factory we're in." Becca took a deep breath and continued. "He called me a little earlier this evening and asked me to meet him here. When I arrived, I saw no one. Came to his office, knocked, and no one answered. The door was ajar, so I started in and found him just as he is now. Then I called 911, and then Joe, the janitor, came in. Can you please tell me if he is alive or not?"

The detective, a male in his fifties, attractive in an offbeat way that would have appealed to Becca under different circumstances, quickly went to the office door and called out, "Sam, how are the medics doing? We have an ID. What's his status?"

The answer came back immediately. "It's a homicide, Ben. Was probably gone before we got here. The ME just arrived and is asking for you."

Becca could feel the nausea rising in her throat, and the tears came, much as she wanted to hide them.

"Were you two romantically involved?" the detective asked softly.

"Not at all," Becca replied hotly. "He has a wife who will have to be told. Two children, a son and a daughter."

"We'll take care of notifying the family. I should introduce myself to you. I'm Detective Ben Hawkins. Will you please wait here while I see to some things in the next room? Will you be all right on your own? We've already had officers searching the factory, and I'll have an officer wait with you. You'll be fine."

"Yes, I can wait here. May I make a phone call?" Becca asked.

"Not just yet, if you don't mind. Give us some time to sort this out a bit. I'll be back in a little while to finish questioning you, and then you'll probably be free to go or call anyone you like."

Becca wasn't sure she liked the sound of that *probably*. All she wanted right now was to hear the reassuring voice of Coach Hightower saying he would come to her and see her through all this.

She could hear the detective outside her door talking to someone. "It's Golden Smith, all right. We knew each other as boys on the circuit going up and down the East Coast. Both our families were what's called MSFWs—migrants and seasonal farmworkers. I've had dealings with him since, when one of his workers did some shit. He was a straight shooter as far as I could tell. I'm sorry he's gone."

"Is there anything in your past together that would fuck up your work on this case?" the second man asked.

"No, it's like I was telling you on the way over. A black dude or dudette is involved, and they pull me in on it. I know there

51

was a lot of talk about me making detective because I'm black. I'm out to prove all those assholes wrong. I'll do fine on this case. Sit back and watch."

"I've been your partner for six months now, and I have no complaints."

Their voices trailed away as they moved farther down the hallway.

Becca was thrown back to a sweltering summer afternoon in Chattanooga. She was riding the bus to go downtown when she noticed a Negro girl about her age sitting all by herself on the crowded bus. It seemed to Becca everyone was avoiding that empty seat beside the black child with people choosing to stand in the overflowing aisles rather than sit next to the little black girl. Becca suddenly wondered what it would feel like to be avoided in that way. From that day on, she was observant of the many ways prejudice showed up in her Southern town.

At Central High, she chose the side for integration in the school's senate debate. Her rival, whose slogan was "Two, four, six, eight; we don't want to integrate!" won the election. However, Becca was elected Miss Central High of 1962, her senior year, due to her inclusive friendliness.

A no-nonsense, sturdily built policewoman entered the small office, almost filling it up to capacity. She nodded to Becca and asked whether she would like any coffee. A patrolman was going out for fortifications.

Becca's stomach rebelled at the very idea of food or drink. She only wanted this to be over. She kept thinking of Golden's two innocent children and how their lives would change. Becca knew firsthand what the early death of a parent could do to a child. At thirteen, she had lost her father when he was only thirty-six, and that was still a wound that festered like a sore tooth that you're able to ignore for the most part but that sometimes just demands your attention. This was one of those times.

The tears threatened to resurface. Becca tried to think of anything other than that beaten body in the next room. And the children.

After a number of minutes had crawled by, the detective in charge reentered the office. "May I have a close look at your hands, Ms. Collins, and with your permission, take a quick photo or two of them?"

"Should I be asking for an attorney, as ridiculous as that sounds to me?" Becca asked.

"Ma'am, you have every right to get an attorney if that is what you think you need at this point," Detective Hawkins replied. "I am not charging you with anything just now. But if it would make you more comfortable, it is certainly your legal right to have representation. Your cooperation will be duly noted in your favor."

Becca tried to make sense of all that was playing out this horrible night and of what this man was saying to her. She knew she had absolutely nothing to hide from the police, and yet, so many TV shows had portrayed perfectly innocent people finding themselves mired in legal quicksand after going it on their own. Becca knew Golden's blood was encrusted on her hands, forearms, and clothes from when she had knelt down to try to stem its heavy flow. Surely this innocent explanation was evident to the police and would ring true with this particular detective.

"Will I be able to leave if you take the pictures?" she asked hesitantly.

"Yes, ma'am, you will after you give us all the pertinent information on how we can get in touch with you. And as long as you agree to appear at the police station at nine tomorrow morning. That will give you tonight to decide if you want an attorney or someone else to come with you—if you feel you need them."

"I appreciate that," Becca replied. "Go ahead. Take your pictures." She was suddenly so tired it was all she could do to get the words out.

Again, the detective seemed to sense her diminished state and gently led her to a chair. The forensics person came in and went to work on her hands. Then the policewoman who had been so silent during their vigil together began asking her the basic questions about where she lived, worked, and the corresponding phone numbers.

She was free to go home. "Will you have any trouble driving?" Detective Hawkins asked her. All Becca wanted was to be far away from this place and these people. "I'll be fine, thank you," she answered, heading for the hallway.

"I'll walk you to your car," the detective stated. Becca was actually glad for this offer, as the thought of the dark factory and parking lot was not making her a happy camper. She wasn't the least bit looking forward to walking through the darkness all alone with a murderer so recently there, maybe even still there.

All the way home, she debated whether or not to call Jack. It would be midnight by the time she reached her cottage. She would have lunch with him the very next day. It would mean everything to her to hear his warm, embracing voice tonight, but she hesitated since he had known her such a short time. Surely she could wait until their lunch and then be able to tell him in person and see his reactions to her dreadful experience. Yes, that would be best. Also, she might know more after her visit to the police station in the morning.

16

Becca woke the next morning amazed that she had experienced a deep and prolonged sleep the night before. She faced two important events today—the visit to the police and the lunch with Jack.

With little trouble, she found the police station in the county office buildings. She arrived early for her nine o'clock appointment. She had chosen a soft pink sweater and gray slacks with much more thought of Jack than the police—although it did cross her mind that she wanted to feel pretty in case Detective Hawkins were back on duty. She was hopeful that she would be so engaged in their conversation that the red terror wouldn't show up and make her look guilty.

She was shown into a small interrogation room with the expected steel table and two folding chairs and a glass mirror that she assumed was one-way. Someone had left a postcard on the table that said "Question Authority" in bold red letters against a black background. She was left alone, so Becca did what she always did when eating alone and waiting for her food—she pulled a blank scrap piece of paper from her purse and started to write down the bills she still had to pay this month versus what was in her checking account, adding in the mileage check she expected next week. For once, the two totals were not that far apart, which Becca took as a good omen for the day.

Detective Hawkins came striding into the room with the look of someone who had been up all night. His paisley tie was just a little crooked. His tan shirt accented his piercing brown eyes, which seemed to approve of her choice of the pink sweater even though there were dark circles underneath those eyes.

"Thank you for coming in this morning, Ms. Collins."

"Is Golden's family all right?" Becca asked anxiously, thinking especially of the children.

"Mrs. Smith is under a doctor's care right now. Her sister is staying with her and helping with the kids," Detective Hawkins answered.

He then took her through the events of last night, step by step. With ease, Becca answered all his detailed questions no matter in what order he placed them. Becca kept her answers short but clear and to the point. She had decided on the ride home last night that she truly had nothing to hide or guard against. She wanted to cooperate as fully as she possibly could, so she decided to go it alone for this first round of questions. She also felt that she was of little help since she had no idea of who was responsible for this brutal killing of her colleague.

After two hours of examination, every detail of the murder was covered from many different angles. Detective Hawkins told her she was free to go about her day. Becca had been worried that the questioning would make her late for her lunch with Jack, but actually, time-wise, everything was falling into place. *Be thankful for small blessings*, she mused.

17

Becca pulled into the school parking lot two minutes early. Jack was waiting for her. He had asked her to be there at 11:52, and it was only 11:50. Becca was so very glad to see him. All sorts of good feelings washed over her. To her great surprise and chagrin, she found herself close to tears.

Jack slipped into the passenger's side and gave her right hand a quick squeeze. He looked handsome in a tan polo shirt with a light green V-necked sweater and tan slacks. Becca was so drawn to him in that moment. All she could think about was the urge to crawl into his arms and stay there until this horror went away.

Jack sensed that Becca was upset. "Let's pull over here and park for a moment. Something has you upset, and I want to hear about it—if you want to tell me."

Becca was happy to comply. The words started tumbling out: her fear last night, the gruesome discovery, her concern for Golden's family, all of it.

Jack let her pour it all out without interruption. Then he said, "You've been through hell these last few hours. Let's put it behind us for now and get some comfort food inside you. Do you feel like driving, or would you like me to take over?"

"Oh, I feel much sturdier now that I've shared it with you," Becca answered. "And we're very close to Friendly's."

"There may be a special treat there for you. I heard the grammar school's kindergarten class is going to be there on a field trip. I have a story I'll share with you once we get seated."

"Great! Can't wait." Becca felt much better than she had in the last twenty-four hours.

They were settled into their cheerful booth when an organized commotion in the back room erupted, and suddenly a stream of five-year-olds marched by their table.

"Good class!" Coach Hightower kept repeating, causing the children to walk taller and puff out their little chests. One tiny girl all decked out in blue to match her eyes turned and gave Becca a stunning smile. Becca returned it in kind and felt her mood lighten even more.

"Wow. That last little boy looks so much like a kid I had last year in football. He played right tackle and was only about 170 pounds. The guy he was up against was at least 235. Just before the game started, I took my kid aside and said, 'That guy is soft. Just keep hitting him in the middle, and he will fold.'"

"Did he fold like you said he would?"

"No, he played a decent game, but my kid played a helluva game—really gave it all he had."

While they continued to wait for their fish sandwiches and french fries, the coach began his tale. Becca loved the wicked sparkle in his eyes.

"A few years back, I first started teaching in Saint Johnsville—friendliest town I ever saw. I would be conducting my phys. ed. class when I got really irritated with what some lazy teachers were doing on my watch. Fifteen minutes or more before their class time with me, these teachers would line the children up outside in the hall. This distracted my current class while the lazy bums were chatting with another teacher down the hall. So I figured out a way to solve the situation.

"I would get that class ready to return to their teacher and classroom by instructing them to create a little surprise for that teacher. I started by asking them if there was anybody in their group who couldn't keep a secret. They would all point to each other, and I would say, 'No, we can't do this unless you all promise to keep it a secret until the person I choose gives you the signal. When that kid does, I want everyone to fire at the sky—or ceiling—to shoot down as many ducks as you can with as much noise as you need to make. Lots of pretend ducks up on your ceiling.

"'Sally, your red hair looks extra pretty today. You can be the signal-giver.' Sally immediately forgot all the teasing she had gotten earlier that day about her freckles.

"'But till Sally gives you the signal, you must be very quiet so you don't scare away all the ducks. You can even go on tiptoe between the gym and your classroom. Got it?'"

"Well, those teachers never knew what hit them! Once they got it figured out, they went to Principal Jones and complained-about me, of all people. He called me in and asked me about it. I told him he must have noticed the commotion in that hallway for a long spell before each class. So we came to an agreement – no more hanging out in my hallway long before class and no more duck shoots."

Becca could just picture all those children suddenly aiming for the sky with all the attendant sound effects! She was so intrigued by the way this man's brain worked and the amount of creativity rattling around in it, she could think of little else. Certainly not dwell on beaten bodies and fatherless children. Not for this precious little while they were together.

The lunch was over all too soon. Coach Hightower was deposited in the busy parking lot next to the high school. Before getting out of the car, he gave Becca some instructions. "Remember who you are. This has nothing to do with you. Call me any time you want to talk."

Becca felt comforted and yet disquieted at the same time, realizing that no future plans were offered by the coach. She felt such a strong connection to him but had no idea if he felt the same way.

It seems to be his nature to be kind and help anyone in trouble. I mustn't assume he's interested in me as a woman, except for that kiss! He's used to being the center of attention—especially where women are concerned. I may not be anyone special to him, just someone who needs a friend right now.

The coach returned to his office marveling at the strength of this lovely woman and how lucky he felt to have her come into his life. He had been focusing on work and family since his wife's unexpected death in a freak car accident four years ago. He was afraid to think long term at the beginning of this friendship, but he already felt a close tie to Becca. His family must come first, though, and his work with the kids, of course.

Still, this was an extra dimension of his life that had been missing. He was lonely when he slowed down enough to admit it. Becca's presence in his life let him know how much he missed having a woman as a companion and partner.

No, I'm thinking too far ahead. Such a beautiful, special woman must have men lined up around the block. I'm just a simple coach, ten years older with two teenage kids. Can't invest too much in this. See how it goes.

18

At the same time, Becca was listening to "Just to be Close to You" by the Commodores on her car radio and wishing she were heading home to the coach that night, along with Rusty Nail.

I need to pay my respects to Mrs. Smith and see how she and the children are doing. And I'll check in with Brick to update him on all this. Plenty to do this afternoon to keep my mind occupied.

When she reached the Sodus office, she was immediately swamped with questions and comments from coworkers.

"Did you know the police have been here asking about you?"

"What was it like finding a dead body?

"Did you know right away that he was dead?"

She ignored and deflected these curiosity seekers and tried to compose her thoughts for the grilling she anticipated from Brick.

He did not disappoint. What surprised her was his intense anger—at her.

"What were you doing going to that deserted factory at eight o'clock at night? What in hell were you thinking? Did you let anyone know where you were going? Well, did you?"

When Becca could get a word in, she informed Brick, "I was doing my job, which I do every night and day under tricky circumstances."

Brick calmed down with that thought. "I apologize for getting so hot under the collar. I just get upset at the idea of you wandering around in the dark with a murderer on the loose! How are you feeling right now? Do you need to take the rest of the day off?"

Becca thought of all that lay ahead that afternoon. "After I bring you up to speed, I really need to reach out to Golden's family. After that, I'll head for home and call it a day."

She proceeded to fill him in on everything she could remember from the dreadful night before and her police experience that morning.

19

An hour later, she headed east to Lyons, New York. As she approached the Smith home, she noticed a black Ford several years old parked alongside the lot of the tidy colonial two-story dwelling. A tricycle had been abandoned on the sidewalk leading to the bright-red front door.

Becca rang the doorbell, and the door was immediately opened by a very efficient-looking black woman several years older than Becca. She was wearing a gray tailored pantsuit that enhanced her air of capability.

"May I help you?" she asked coolly but politely.

"I'm a friend of Noreen's and Golden's," Becca replied. "I simply want to express my sympathy to Noreen and the children. Also, I was there last night and thought Noreen might have some questions I could help her with. My name is Becca Collins."

"You were there last night. Are you with the police, then?" The woman looked at her skeptically.

"No, I had a business appointment with Golden at the time the incident occurred. I don't want to intrude if this is a bad time. But I would like to come in and speak with Noreen if she isn't resting."

"I'll check with my sister. Please wait here."

Becca was left standing outside Golden's home on the doorstep in a yard that was deserted in the late-afternoon sun.

In just a little while, the sister returned. "Noreen will see you for a few moments. Please come in."

Becca entered the hallway and walked past a family room that held a television on low volume tuned in to a *Captain Kangaroo* broadcast. Two children around four and six years old appeared to be transfixed by the gentle man entertaining them.

The two women continued on to a formal living room where Noreen Smith was waiting. Becca found herself impressed with the orderliness of this room considering the ages of two of the young family members with access to it.

"Noreen, I am so very sorry. Is there anything I can do for you or for the children?" Becca asked.

"Becca, I'm very glad you came to visit us. I'm still numb from it all. I don't understand how it happened—how he's gone! Just this time yesterday, he called me to say he would be a little later than usual, that he was meeting you after hours but that it was important. I teased him about what a hardship it must be to work late with such a beautiful woman, but he didn't have his usual snappy answer. He sounded really worried about something. Said he couldn't go into it over the phone but would tell me all about it when he got home. I wish now I had pressed him to tell me a little more. I don't know what to think. I just don't know."

Becca moved over to be beside her on the overstuffed brown leather couch, but her sister reached Noreen first.

"I don't think this is helping Noreen. I think you should leave."

"Oh, Mavis, no, I'll pull myself together. Becca has come all this way, and she may be able to help me figure this hellish mess out."

"Whatever you want, Noreen, but you do need to get some rest before Mother gets here."

"Don't remind me," Noreen said ruefully. She turned to Becca as Mavis left the room, explaining, "My whole family is known to close ranks quickly when any member is in trouble. Excuse the military jargon—my father was a career marine, God rest his soul. And Mother is just as strong under pressure."

"So you came by your poise under fire honestly," Becca replied.

"I suppose so." Noreen sighed. "Becca, who could have done this? I know the growers aren't happy with Golden's efforts but, surely they wouldn't be behind something this evil! What do you think?"

"To tell you the truth, Noreen, I am beyond thoughts on all this. It is just too hard. And too sad. How are the children doing?"

"They are asking when Daddy is coming home. Mother will help me with them, and maybe his funeral will make it all more real for them. We'll figure out the arrangements when Mother gets here. If you'll excuse me, I think I'll go rest a bit till she comes. I hope you understand. It was good of you to come."

"Of course I understand," Becca replied, feeling at a loss for anything helpful to say to the grieving woman. "Please give my best to your mother and my thanks to your sister. Take care of yourself, Noreen."

Becca let herself out, saying a quick good-bye to the children, who responded politely and then quickly returned to the solace of public television's children's programming, currently a *Tom and Jerry* cartoon.

20

The ride west was enhanced by a multicolored panorama of fall foliage that barely registered with Becca. She arrived home to find Rusty Nail lolling in the windowsill, all limbs akimbo like a *Playboy* bunny posing for the magazine's centerfold. The answering machine was blinking away and revealed several calls from newspaper reporters in nearby Rochester. She decided to ignore them for the time being.

Tomorrow was a big day on several counts, the main one being the arrival of the new staff member, Jo Lombardi, the political appointment. For some reason, Becca already felt on the defensive with this new coworker, as though Lombardi's status were somehow superior due to her political pull.

Really, right this minute, Jo Lombardi is the least of my worries! she thought as she snuggled deep under the bedcovers. Rusty Nail fit his soft body into the curve of her back, and they safely drifted off to sleep, unaware of all that the darkness held.

Need a few more drinks to relax and get some sleep. Want to be on the alert tomorrow, 'cause the time is coming to put an end to that holier-than-thou bitch. She's just like all the others. Just like my ma! All these women pretending to be all sweet on the outside when there's nothing but rottenness on the inside. Always throwing themselves at any man who passes by but—oh, God—just let a man have some power and watch them spread their legs as fast as they can! My ma hopped in bed with every crew boss that crossed her path. Didn't matter how much my pa beat her after. And who knows if that man is really my dad? I sure as hell don't. And every time she'd fuck the crew boss, he would turn on me and give me the shittiest jobs or dock my pay for no reason. Up and down the East Coast, it was the same every season, every crew boss. I hated that woman's guts!

I would have finished off my woman, but I think the little one needs her. Have a soft spot for that baby child. But I got rid of the big power man she's been putting out for. And I'll get rid of this slutty tramp before she has a chance to two-time her next unlucky bastard.

Those growers knew I was listening when they said that uppity bitch needs to be taught a lesson. I'm just the man to do it. Messing with my family, getting women to take men's jobs. My job.

21

The next morning, Becca made an extra effort to get to the Sodus office a little before nine. However, a woman was already there waiting for her. The woman's most striking feature was the scar tissue remaining after a bad burn on the left side of her face. Makeup only drew one's attention to the area. Becca, of course, tried to not stare at this part of her face but to focus on the woman's eyes, a lovely shade of green. She walked forward, hand outstretched, and introduced herself.

"I'm Becca Collins. You must be Jo. We've been looking forward to your joining us."

"Yes, I'm Josie Lombardi, reporting for duty. Looking forward to working with you too."

The formalities over, Becca led the way to the small multipurpose conference room in the back of the office, ignoring the curious stares and muted whispers of the rest of the local staff.

"Let's settle in at this table, and I'll run through the reason we're here and our strategies for achieving our goals. In a little while, I'll take you around our home base, this office, and introduce you to those who work here full-time. As I'm sure you were told, most of our time is spent in the field, the thirteen counties in the middle of New York State. But let's start with you telling me a little about yourself, your background, and what has led you to take this job."

Josie hesitated, gathering her thoughts. She spoke slowly at first, haltingly, and then the words tumbled out on their own. "This is my first try at working since the fire at my home seven years ago. No one was killed. I went back in to bring out my fourteen-year-old cat, Sunkist, and a section of the roof caved in, trapping us until the firemen reached us. I suffered burns over a third of my body and underwent four operations to get back to myself as much as I have. I know it's hard to look at me. I just can't keep hiding away from the rest of the world any longer. I've been volunteering for years in various capacities for the Democrats, and a dear friend offered me this opportunity. Do you think we can get the work done, or do you see me as a hindrance?"

Thinking of Rusty Nail, Becca asked, "Sunkist isn't still with you, is she?"

"No, she made it two more years, thankfully."

"I'm glad you gave her two more years of life. I'm sorry it was at such a heavy price. Josie, I appreciate your sharing so much with me this morning. Absolutely, we can get the work done—we're a team. And I value your courage and your determination; they will come in handy on this job. I have to tell you, you're getting here at a tricky time, so there won't be quite as much attention paid to you as there would have been. We are all distracted by a murder that occurred only a few days ago. I had the dubious honor of discovering the victim's body—he was a friend of mine with whom I had a business appointment set up for that night. So if you get any strange reactions from the staff, their minds may be elsewhere. Just try to bear with us."

"How awful for you! I'm so sorry!" Josie exclaimed.

Becca could feel the sincerity of the empathy being extended and made an effort to stay strong. Her resentment over having been left out of the hiring process was dissipating quickly.

Just then, Lillian, the receptionist, stuck her head into their conference room. "Becca, excuse me, but Brick needs to talk to you right away. He wants you to go to a private office. Bill Warden is out today. You can use his office."

"Thanks, Lillian." She turned to Josie. "Josie, please look over these flyers and pamphlets and be thinking of how they strike you and how we could improve them for our public. I'll be right back."

She hurried to Bill's office to take Brick's call. She closed the door behind her. "Brick, I really like Josie already and think we'll do a really good job together."

"Fine. Fine," he said dismissively. "We are about to get hit with a nationally publicized situation. You will be entertaining a visitor with a public following who loves to make trouble. Not since Bobby Kennedy came to visit the camps have we been faced with such a high-profile visitor. It's up to you to be the perfect representative of our program, of our agency, and still keep trouble from happening."

"Brick, who in the world is coming here and why?" Becca asked.

"The supremely self-important Reverend Joe Turner is coming tomorrow. He has never missed an opportunity to be on camera. He is coming to make his pronouncements about Golden's death in particular and maybe migrants and seasonal farmworkers in general."

"Tomorrow? Tomorrow when?" Becca broke in, overwhelmed by all that was happening.

"We're still getting the details nailed down," Brick answered. "I'll call back when I know. I just want you to clear the decks and be ready for anything. Give Josie a chair and a copy of Judge Richey's Court Order to read and any other busywork you can come up with to keep her completely out of the line of fire. Stay close to this phone for the next few hours until we get this set up. I'm sure the top brass will show up from Rochester. I'm probably going to drive over from Albany, so it's not all on your shoulders. I'm just giving you a heads-up to clear the day and be thinking about which camps would be our best success stories in case he sticks around long enough to look at one or two. He did ask for you specifically, knowing you were at the scene and found Golden's body. Just be prepared. Be careful in what you say, as it may end up on the national news. Gotta go. I'll call back shortly. Hang in there."

The line went dead in Becca's hand.

She hurried back to where Josie was waiting patiently. "That was our supervisor. I believe you'll be seeing him here tomorrow. However, you may have to entertain yourself tomorrow with the help of some material I'll give you to go over. We've been told we'll have a very high-profile visitor in connection with the murder I told you about. I will be needed to help hold his hand while he's here. Brick will call back with more details as he gets them."

"You know, I had a doctor's appointment that I haven't yet canceled till I spoke with you. I felt funny asking for a sick day my second day on the job, but maybe it would work out better for all of us if I follow through on the appointment and leave you free to handle this unexpected visitor. What do you think?"

"That's perfect. I was feeling lousy about not being with you tomorrow. You do your thing, and we'll do ours, and I'll give you all the juicy details on Wednesday. Now let's talk about our mission."

The rest of the morning passed matter-of-factly, with Becca keeping an ear out for Brick's next call. Lunchtime posed a problem, as they would have to drive to the nearest food supply source and thus be away from the phone. Becca decided to be proactive and give Brick a call to clear their way to lunch. Priorities.

"Just as I thought, Cliff and John will arrive at the Sodus office about nine in the morning. The Rev. is supposed to make his grand appearance at ten or thereabouts. The press will set up any time they want to, so alert the staff to be ready with 'No comment!' as they arrive for work. I'll be heading out in a little while and may catch you before you leave for the day. Meet Josie. This is a hell of a way to start a job."

"It would be great if you make it here in time to meet her. She has a medical appointment tomorrow, so we decided it would work well if she just takes a sick day and we start fresh on Wednesday."

"Good plan, Becca. One less variable to worry about. See you in a few hours."

"Thanks, Brick."

A feeling of relief washed over her at the thought of Brick's coming that very day.

"Josie, let's head out. Have you ever eaten at Orbaker's up on 104?"

"Nope. I'm up for trying it, though. One of your favorites?"

"Most definitely!"

Over lunch, Becca shared with Josie what had brought her to the New York State Department of Labor. "It was a combination of things. I was looking for work and not finding it, so I headed for the Department of Labor's employment office.

All they had to offer was a temporary three-month job with themselves. The woman interviewing me said she didn't think it would be a good match for a woman—that it was working with migrants and often at night when they were home at the camps, possibly dangerous places. I'm a Southern girl who has always had a soft spot for the underdog. I figure we are all an underdog at some time or another, and I've always been concerned about how our country, most especially my South, has treated black people. I wanted to go with the Freedom Riders to help register voters in the Deep South, but parental permission was required by my school, and my mother wouldn't give it. I now realize she was concerned about my safety. At the time, I was very angry with her and thought that possibly prejudice was playing a role in her decision. Yet, she's the one who taught me to try to be of service to the disadvantaged. We're all such a mixed bag!"

"So, after seeing *Harvests of Shame* a few years ago, Edward R. Murrow's piece, the migrants have been a group of people I've been concerned about. This job seemed a perfect opportunity to be of help to them. It was an idealistic thought, but I think some good has come of it."

"Have you lost some of that idealism?" Josie asked her.

"It depends on which day you're asking me. I think some of the edges of it have worn off, but the core conviction is still there."

22

fter a very satisfying hamburger, the overflowing contents of which made their way down the front of both Becca's and Josie's tops, they left the busy Orbaker's and headed back on 104 to the Department of Labor office just down Route 88.

As they pulled into the office's parking lot, the increased activity was noticeable. There were actual camera crews from two of the local news networks setting up outside the office building and also two police cars parked at an angle to the front door.

"Looks like they're getting ready to arrest someone or something big is happening," Josie commented.

Becca suddenly got a queasy feeling in the pit of her stomach. Why would the police cars be here at her place of work? And two of them? It looked so official with the marked police cars in place. Becca quickly ran through her interview with Detective Hawkins and couldn't think of any reason she should worry. Or so she hoped.

"We'd better go in, shouldn't we?" Josie asked hesitantly, interrupting Becca's mental gymnastics.

"Yes, I just need to go straight through the press setup and remember 'No comment.' You too."

"Certainly," Josie replied. "You lead, and I will follow."

They got out of the car and made their way to the front door of the office. Flashbulbs popped, and microphones were pushed in their faces.

"Is either of you two Becca Collins?"

"Is it true you found the badly beaten body? Could you tell right away that he was dead? Was there much blood? Were you afraid?"

"Is it true you and Golden were having an affair, and he wanted to end it?"

The last question came from a short blonde woman in a powder-blue suit standing in front of one of the cameras from a Rochester station. Becca turned toward her, every bit of her wanting to ask this woman where in the world she had gotten such an idea. Josie put her hand on Becca's arm.

"No comment," Becca managed to say as they made it to the office building. Just then, a police officer in uniform opened the front door and hustled them inside.

Becca was both a little surprised and somewhat relieved to see Detective Hawkins across the room speaking with Lillian, the receptionist. That relief quickly turned to apprehension, as she could think of no good reason for the police to be here at her place of work.

Lillian looked over and spotted Becca and Josie. "They're here now. I'd better get back to the phones," she said, and she hurried away.

Detective Hawkins turned toward them and held out his hand to Josie. "Let me introduce myself. I'm Detective Ben Hawkins, in charge of the investigation into the murder of Golden Smith. And you are ...?"

"I'm Josie Lombardi, Becca Collins's second in command. This is my first day of work for New York State, and I never had the occasion to meet Mr. Smith."

"Okay. We would appreciate a brief statement to that effect, which you can give to the policewoman just through that first door. Thank you."

Josie gave Becca's arm a quick squeeze and hastened in the direction the detective had indicated.

"Now, Miss Collins, we have a few more questions for you, if you don't mind. I've asked to use the conference room for a few hours, so we can go in there."

Becca followed him down the hallway, very much aware of being the focus of all eyes in the office, even though several of her coworkers were engaged in conversations with various uniformed officers. Her mind was racing. Was this the result of not having gotten an attorney to be with her yesterday morning at the police station? Should she quickly come up with one now? Or was it already too late?

"I'm not sure what's happening here," she told the detective, "but maybe I should get legal representation."

"You have that right. However, your full cooperation would be looked on favorably. It's your call."

"Can you tell me why you and all your other officers are here? I doubt that Golden was ever in this office more than two or three times."

"I can't really comment on the investigation to you at this time. Won't you sit down? We'll get through this as quickly as possible and let you get back to your work."

It was so tempting to simply go along with this man, whom, up to this point, she liked and respected. It sounded so reasonable to continue to cooperate, as she had nothing to hide. But the television reporter's question had put Becca a little more on the alert and a lot more on the defensive. "I think I would like to get an attorney's help before answering any more of your questions," she stated none too firmly.

"Then I would like you and your attorney to be at the police station at four today. No later. I will meet you there. We're done here." He quickly turned away from her and headed back to the main office area. As he left the building, the reporters tried to get answers from him, but he easily brushed past them to his police car, his partner close behind.

23

Becca was shaking all over when Josie came in and found her in tears. Becca quickly pulled herself together and asked Josie, "Do you know any good criminal lawyers? I need one now."

Josie replied, "You're joking, right?"

"No jokes today. I'll call my friend Karen Morrison. She's an assistant DA, and she'll know what to do. I hope." Becca shook her head.

"How do you know her?"

"We've worked together on the battered women's shelter in Williamson. She's a wonderful person and a very quick thinker. If I can reach her, I'll be ok."

"Come to your desk where the phone is. I'll think of things to say to Brick when he gets here if you're still talking to Karen," Josie offered.

"Oh my God! Everything is happening at once—although I guess there's no convenient time to be suspected of murder. What an intro this has been for you, Josie."

"Don't you worry for one minute about me. You just get with your friend the attorney, and you two will figure this out. We Italians can take care of ourselves. Make your call. I'll go in the kitchen back there and make you a cup of tea."

"That sounds perfect," Becca replied gratefully.

When Josie brought out the cup of tea, Becca gave her report. "Karen had the name of an excellent defense lawyer who is rearranging some things to meet me at the police station at four. I'm feeling much better. This is all just a ridiculous mistake. It will work out—I just know it will."

"I couldn't agree more," Josie replied. "I was thinking that we should put our thinking caps on and see if there are any plausible leads you could share with the police. You know, steer them in another direction."

"It's just beyond me to think of possibilities at this moment. But Golden was known for taking on the power structure."

"The power structure being ...?"

"The growers, of course," Becca replied. "I don't think it's up to me to solve this murder," she continued. "But I'll give it some thought."

"It would be worth it, Becca, to give it a lot of thought. Would you be able to focus better at home? I can hold the fort here till Brick arrives."

"I feel so guilty leaving you here. But it might really help clear these cobwebs if I did go home and meditate for a few minutes. If you're sure you are okay, I think I'll take you up on your offer. Thank you, Josie. You've been wonderful!"

24

several hours later after the police interview, a bone-tired Becca was unlocking her little home's door when she heard a car approaching. Amazingly, it was Coach Hightower—the one person she wanted to be with no matter how weary she was.

"I've been hearing snippets of news on the radio, and I know this has been a horrendous day for you. I just wanted to see you in person to see how you are and to give you a hug. I'll leave right now if you want me to."

"Oh, Jack, I am so happy to see you! Please come in, and I'll collect that hug."

"It's all yours for the asking. My kids are nicely occupied for the next little while, so I'm at your disposal. But you have to agree to kick me out when you feel like it."

"I'll agree to anything to get you in my house."

"I like the sound of that. Let me help you with your jacket, and then you can bring me up to speed on this mess."

Becca happened to have a bottle of wine on hand that she had purchased two days ago with a lot of hope that this very scenario would occur. They settled in on the couch with Rusty Nail checking out the coach's shoes for foreign creatures' scents.

Becca ran through the day's events as quickly as she could, ending with this latest session at the police station. Her attorney had swiftly advised her to not say any more to the police until they could find out where the idea of an affair had come from.

"I know you haven't known me that long," Becca continued, "but I promise you that nothing of a romantic nature ever occurred between Golden and me. I even know his wife and children and would never dream of hurting a family like them."

"I may not have known you long, but I feel I am a good reader of people. I completely and easily believe you," Jack assured her, taking her hand in his.

"Let's talk about you for a nice change. How did your day go?"

"Well, it was the usual. The kids were great. A parent showed up as I was leaving with the same old question: 'How come my kid doesn't get more playing time?'"

"Do you have to tell them the brutal truth, or do you sugarcoat it a bit, depending on the parent and the kid?"

"Oh no, that question is absolutely no problem for me. I just refer them back to their kid. He knows."

"I would think most kids in their early teens are not that self-aware," Becca commented.

"My kids know exactly where they stand. We have a system. As you probably know, there are two tackles on each side. So for one side, there may be four kids wanting two spots. Numbers one and two are the ones playing. Then there's number three and number four. If four feels he is up to the task, he can challenge number three. If he wins the challenge, then next time, he can challenge number two and move up to play the next game. If not successful, he is well aware that he is number three and won't be getting playing time as long as numbers one and two stay healthy. So you don't hear the kids complaining—they know exactly where they stand. And I encourage them after the challenge—tell them what they've improved since the last challenge and what they can work on before the next challenge. It keeps everybody on their toes," Jack concluded.

"It sounds so fair!" Becca exclaimed. Her admiration and respect for Jack increased each time they had a conversation. And she realized she hadn't been thinking of herself at all while listening to Jack and learning about his system.

"You've had a long day," Jack said, drawing her into his arms. "Is there anything I can do for you tomorrow to lighten your load?"

"You're helping me so much right this minute. I love knowing that I can count on you to listen to me and support me through this mess."

"You've got it. I'm sorry I have to leave now. Time disappears when I'm with you, Becca. You have definitely improved my life these last few weeks. I'm so sorry you have to go through such an ordeal. But 'this too will pass,' as my mother always said."

"Jack, I could certainly understand if you wanted to rethink our friendship or put it on pause till I get beyond this. There will be some nasty publicity, and people will be talking. It could spill over on you. You know how people are with gossip."

"Yes, I do know how people are, but I like to make up my own mind, and my mind and the rest of me are very happy to know you. You get my vote, kid. We'll get through this together. But no more talk tonight." With that, he took Becca in his arms and gave her a toe-tingling kiss and then headed for the door. "Be sure you lock it behind me," he instructed her.

Wisely, it turned out. The watcher hidden fifty yards from them in the apple orchard was disappointed that he had wasted the evening waiting for the coach to leave. The rusty wrench he had found on the floor of his truck struck and banged against the palm of his hand. He imagined its connection to the strawberry-blonde troublemaker's head. A sudden cloudburst further discouraged him from carrying out any plans for the no-count do-gooder as he hurried back to where he had hidden his truck. He cursed the rain, the coach, and that interfering woman.

She'll get hers—the time just has to be right.

Snug inside the comfy cottage, Becca checked Rusty Nail's water dish and prepared for bed. She wanted to be as alert as possible for the morning's encounter with the Reverend Joe Turner. She set her alarm for the early awakening and fell into a deep sleep while thinking amorous thoughts of Coach Hightower.

But not before troublesome thoughts came and went about this budding relationship. She felt so at ease with the coach. Would this continue when they became more involved on a sexual level? They were taking it slowly, very slowly, which suited her, she guessed. She was not sure whose choice it was to be so careful. One day at a time. There were a lot of ladies to plow through to get his attention, but it was well worth it. She was so very grateful for his presence in her life at this difficult time. That should be enough for her for now.

25

The next morning, Becca checked in with Rusty Nail on her choice of attire for the day. She felt the need for her black blazer with black slacks and a soft red blouse as an understated power outfit.

She was unhappily aware of the car that closely followed her all the way to the Sodus office. Two camera crews were already getting into place as she arrived. She hurried past them into the reception area where she was overwhelmed with relief at the sight of Brick joking with Lillian. She was not the only one who had come in early this morning, either for the hope of camera time or Brick time. Becca wasn't sure which.

Brick was his usual handsome self in a casual yet impressive and fashionable denim suit, sporting a fresh haircut and an impeccably trimmed beard. His cowboy boots had received a fresh shine for the occasion.

Becca found herself looking for the comforting presence of Josie until she remembered her doctor's appointment for that day. Becca was curious to find out if Brick's impression of Josie would match her own.

"I am so glad to see you, Brick. Any sign of our visitor yet?"

"No, I wanted to catch you before the circus begins. Glad you made it in this early after the day you had yesterday," Brick greeted her.

"I'm doing okay," Becca demurred. "Brick, what did you think of Josie? Did you two spend some quality time together yesterday afternoon? I was so sorry to not be here to introduce you two."

"Well, she's sold on getting to work with you, that's for sure. I think she's a quality lady and will be a solid contributor to your team, to our team."

"I'm very glad we're in agreement about Josie. I'm definitely looking forward to working with her and getting to know her better."

"And you're so hard to get along with," Brick teased. "I guess I have my hands full with two females as my staff. I'll just have to figure out how to make the best of it."

"I'm sure you'll manage just fine," Becca retorted.

Just then, there was noticeable activity around the entryway. A group made its entrance, and it was obvious who the top dog was. Reverend Joe Turner was a commanding presence in his well-tailored brown pinstripe suit with an apricot-paisley tie and accent handkerchief in his pocket. He was tall and slender, and Becca noticed a slight limp as he entered the office.

Brick hurried forward to greet the reverend. Flashbulbs popped and captured the two main players in this drama. Becca held back and waited to see when Brick would require her presence. He was in the process of getting introduced to various members of the entourage when he motioned for Becca to join them.

"Rev. Turner, this is Becca Collins, our Rural Manpower Representative under Judge Richey's Court Order. She happened to be the person who found Golden Smith's body that fateful night. Becca, this is Rev. Joe Turner. He has come to weigh in on the situation."

The reverend looked a little taken aback by Brick's description of the reason for his presence. "I have come to bring solace to the grieving widow and the fatherless children and to make sure the system operates as it should, with fairness and justice for all concerned."

"That is what we are all striving for," Becca said smoothly. "I'm glad to meet you and will be happy to assist you in any way I can during your visit."

Brick's colleague, Cliff, and his second in command, John, strode in the front door and marched over to their little group.

Introductions were made all around again. Becca noticed a pronounced coolness from the Rochester contingent to the reverend and his group.

A representative from one of the TV stations approached them, wanting to set things up for the cameras. "We want the reverend in the center of the shot, of course, as he gives his comments, and the lady who found the body to be on his left. Who's highest in the Department of Labor's chain of command here?"

"Well, it's kind of apples and oranges," Cliff tried explaining. "Brick here is Albany staff in charge of a special unit for outreach to migrants and seasonal farmworkers. I'm a little higher up the ladder when it comes to the traditional Rural Manpower Reps. By the way, I just heard they may be changing our title to Rural Employment Representative—some political correctness nonsense!"

"Oh, that's interesting," the TV guy said, not very convincingly. "Let's set up outside the building where the light is good."

They all trooped out into the bright sunlight. Becca was on the outside of the lineup, and then the reverend, and then the interviewer with Cliff and Brick on his right. Becca hadn't expected to feel the heat from the lights that were trained on them despite it being broadcast in broad daylight.

"Rev. Turner, can you tell us what brings you all the way out to Wayne County from New York City? And what are your thoughts about this terrible murder that has occurred?"

"Well, of course, we don't have all the facts in yet, and we wouldn't want to rush to judgment. But I'm concerned about the climate out here created by the growers that encourages and even condones violence against those that try to help the downtrodden and disadvantaged and against the very workers themselves."

"Could you be more specific? Do you have any evidence that a grower was involved in this crime?"

"I'm speaking to a culture that breeds violence—the use of crew bosses and the methods they use to keep workers 'in line.' From all I hear, Golden Smith was not a man who would stay in line—or get in line, for that matter. He was a leader and an innovator, and he shouldn't have been struck down in the middle of his mission. You can figure out who it was that wanted him stopped."

"That's not our job, Reverend," the reporter shot back. "Do you have any evidence or information that would shed light on this situation?"

"I am here to give solace and support to the widow and the children and to say to the world out there that we will not stand by quietly when good men are struck down in the night by cowards and cutthroats. We are here to be one with our brothers and sisters, the migrants and farmworkers who pick our crops and put the food on our very tables."

He stepped back to allow Cliff access to the microphone. Cliff couldn't have looked more uncomfortable during Rev. Turner's exchange with the reporter. He hesitated and then introduced himself as a representative of the New York State Department of Labor. "As the reverend said, we certainly do not have all the facts yet—in fact, we know very little about what actually happened Tuesday night. It could have been a random mugging for all we know. We mustn't jump to any conclusions. Brick, did you or Becca have anything to add?"

"No," Brick answered, "except that we do need to keep an open mind and let the police do their jobs."

"Is this the lady who found the body?" a second reporter asked.

Brick put his arm under Becca's elbow and moved her to the center of the group. She appreciated the support but not the nudge to have the spotlight shined on her.

"Yes, I found Golden in his office. We had an eight o'clock appointment to discuss employee problems." Becca had decided to not bring Rose's name into this conversation, if the grilling from the press could be called that.

"Any particular employee he was having problems with?" The reporter wasn't going to let her off that easy.

"I didn't have the opportunity to find out what was troubling him," Becca replied. That seemed to satisfy the inquisitors for the moment.

Cliff stepped forward and ended the session. Becca felt a wave of relief wash over her as they turned to go back inside.

"That was good strategy, Becca, to give them something to think about other than the damn growers," Cliff praised her as they reentered the office building.

"It certainly wasn't strategy on my part," retorted Becca. "Just the truth as I know it."

"And the truth shall set you free!" Reverend Turner interjected. Cliff seemed to have forgotten his presence for a moment. "You appear to be a straight shooter, young woman. Will you be accompanying me on my camp visits today?"

"I'll be happy to, Reverend. How much time do you have to spend on these visits? That will help us to determine which camps we see; as you may know, they are quite spread out. Or is there a certain number that you have in mind? Or a specific camp? We do have to obtain the growers' permission to go on their land."

"I'll just bet you have chosen carefully and well regarding what I will see. I am in your hands. You lead the way."

Becca detected a twinkle in his eye as he spoke to her and sensed a keen intelligence behind all his folksy manner.

I'll stay on my toes, but this might not be such a painful afternoon, after all, she told herself with wonder.

26

As it turned out, Becca became more and more impressed with the questions Rev. Turner asked and the concern and care with which he asked them. He then listened thoughtfully to their answers. He was much more subdued when dealing with the farmworkers, almost gentle in his handling of them. Of course, most of the workers were enmeshed in their work of getting the apples down from the trees and into their canvas bags to be poured into the bushel baskets waiting among the trees, but many took a small break to speak with this stranger in a suit who had the same skin color as they did.

"Where is your home base? I know that part of Florida well."

"How many children do you have back home?"

"How long has it been since you've seen your family?"

"Are you able to send much of your pay down home? Not as much as you had hoped to send, I'll bet. Keep up the good work. Keep your eye on the prize. You'll get home to those four children very soon."

Becca had gotten prior permission from the specific growers to allow Rev. Turner and Becca to go on their land and visit their camps and even to speak to "their" workers. The Brownings were gracious about it, and two other growers begrudgingly said yes, if it would help the situation. They just hoped it wouldn't stir up more trouble.

One grower who had obviously had too much to drink waved a gun in Becca's face when she made her request. She made a hasty retreat and noted not to return to that farm in the future.

Luckily for Becca, the reverend had another speaking commitment that night in Rochester and could only fit in two nearby visits, which appeared to go smoothly.

As his entourage drove west, Becca reflected on how often in her short life preconceived ideas of people had been upended the more she got to know the person in question.

Reverend Turner definitely fit in that group. She would pay more attention to his pronouncements in the future, no longer summarily dismissing him as a troublemaker.

27

Becca knew Brick would want a full account of their visits. She hoped that she could then connect with Jack and run the events of this day by him if he were available for her call. An in-person visit would be even better.

She felt bold enough to drop by the high school on her way back to the office. She made her way to the athletic area. She could hear laughter as she drew near.

"You're such a kidder!" an attractive fortysomething woman was exclaiming as Becca hesitated just outside the doorway. The enticing smell of chocolate brownies reached her. Jack noticed her standing there and waved her in.

"I don't want to interrupt," Becca said haltingly, feeling foolish to have expected Jack to be totally at her disposal. The familiar sense of not being welcomed by those already present stopped her from crossing the threshold.

"Not at all, Becca. I'm so glad to see you. Come in. Have a brownie. They're homemade."

The other woman was looking her over and was not as happy to see her as Jack was. "I guess I'd better get back to my desk," she said coolly.

"Thanks again for the brownies," Jack told her.

"They are for you and your children," she said pointedly.

"I know they will love them. They always do," Jack replied.

"Nice meeting you," Becca said, although they hadn't really met at all.

The other woman made no reply; just left, which was fine with Becca.

"How did you do with your big-city visitor?" Jack asked warmly.

"Well, the reverend wasn't exactly what I was expecting," Becca started explaining.

The telephone rang, and Jack held up his hand in apology as he answered it. The conversation was brief. However, two students burst in talking excitedly about a stolen moped, followed by two more women who made a beeline to the brownies and to Jack.

Becca felt defeated at that point and in no condition to vie for Jack's attention. "I'll check in with you later when you're not so busy," she told him as she turned to the door.

"Becca, wait." Jack crossed the room quickly and put his hand on her arm. Her reaction to his touch was immediate and intense. "Please let me stop by tonight if you're not at the camps, and we can trade war stories about our day. I should be able to shake free and be at your house about 7:30. Make that 7:32. I go by train time. Learned that from the West Point coach when I was up there for a clinic last summer."

"That would be great," she answered, relieved and excited at the thought of time alone together with him.

28

At 7:32 on the dot, Jack was at her door. She felt an overwhelming rush of comfort at the sight of him, along with fierce pangs of desire. He was dressed in khaki slacks and a turquoise-blue golf shirt open at the throat, which accentuated his outdoor tan and sparkling green eyes.

"Please come in." Becca was suddenly aware she hadn't been concentrating on her housekeeping duties the last few days. Her comfortable living room held various stacks of books and mail that had to be within reach for when she was ready to examine them more carefully.

"Wasn't that quite a thunderstorm we had last night?" Jack asked as he entered her home. "My neighbor was so scared she wanted to come spend the night with me. I told her we'd be a little crowded, as Marcie's friend was over for the night. Luckily, the storm passed on, so she needn't have worried."

"That was good luck!" Becca answered dryly. "May I get you a cup of tea or some wine?"

"A cup of tea would be perfect. Can I help you with anything?"

"No, I'll just be a minute. Say hello to Rusty Nail, and make yourself comfortable."

Becca was setting up the teapot when Rusty Nail wandered into the kitchen. "If a nude woman stretched out in front of him, he would ask her, 'Are you chilly? Can I get you a blanket?'" Becca complained to Rusty Nail, who was busy concentrating on carefully cleaning between each toe. Rusty Nail did not deign to answer her.

The teapot whistled happily, and Becca prepared a tray with mugs and a plate of Oreo cookies, which she carried into the living room.

"Just what I needed—a bracing cup of tea!" Jack exclaimed as he helped her settle the tray on her scarred wooden chest that served as a coffee table. "First of all, is there anything new on the police front?"

"I'm hoping no news is good news," Becca answered abruptly, hoping to change the subject from the frightening police happenings. She proceeded to share with Jack all the ups and downs of her day, including her revamped opinion of

Rev. Joe Turner. Through her recitation, she sensed that Jack was waiting his turn to share something with her that he was excited about.

"Okay, now it's your turn, Jack. You seem excited by something, something good, and I want to hear what it is," Becca coaxed.

"You seem to know me pretty well—I do have something good to share. This fall, in addition to everything else I do as athletic director, I've decided to set up a wrestling program at Riverside High. I'm so excited about it because it allows the little guys in school—those who haven't a chance to make the football team, the basketball team, or the baseball team and those who can't make the track team—not long enough strides—to compete and win. The small guys are so quick and able to easily make the switches in wrestling. It really gives them something to shoot for.

"Just today, in front of his whole gym class, I put my arm around the shoulders of this one small kid and said, 'Just think. You could be the Wayne County champion.' You should have seen the look on that kid's face. It was priceless! I know this program's going to do a lot of good. Think of the potential scholarships."

"Oh, Jack, you're worth your weight in gold to that high school and to the county and its kids. Thank you so much for letting me know about it. What a great way to end this day."

"Sharing it with you makes it all the better for me too, Becca. But before you go putting me up there in the 'great guy' category, let me tell you what your hero did last night." Jack placed his mug on the table/chest and turned to her, seated beside him on the couch. "Michael's home for his break, and Marcie was all excited about cooking for her men, so I made it a point to be there and let us all have supper together. I was telling them about this amazing catch one of my boys did. Michael said, 'Did you see my pass to Brian and the way I got around Jeffrey to make it?'

"I stupidly answered, 'No, I don't watch you, Michael. I watch the other guys.'

"'Well,' he said, 'Just like in high school!' and got up from the table and went outside into the woods behind our house. Marcie said, 'Oh, Dad, how could you?' and got up and went after him. I had to go back to school and didn't see either of them again until this morning when we barely spoke to each other."

Becca sat quietly, fully understanding the hurt Michael had felt at his father's supposed indifference. She was an unwilling participant in the distance Jack had described with his children. "So what are you doing here now?" she asked him.

He pulled back, stung and somewhat surprised by her coolness. "I just wanted to check on you and give you a hug and a kiss. If you mean why am I not with the kids, they'll be there when I get home. You're my priority right this minute."

"I appreciate that," Becca said stiffly, feeling more alone than before he had arrived. "I would feel better, though, if you were straightening out things with Michael and Marcie, especially since he's here for a short time. We can get together a few days from now." Her voice broke. The redness had begun creeping up her neck and into her face.

"That sounds like a long time away. But if you want me to go, of course I'll go. I know it's been a long day for you."

"Yes."

"May I at least kiss you good night?"

"Of course."

He reached for her and drew her into the warm embrace of his arms. Becca knew she was not melting into him as she had before. Still, their lips found each other, and their breaths intermingled as one. His tongue tantalizingly outlined her lips and mouth. She pulled back.

"I'll try to reach you at your office sometime during the day tomorrow if that's okay with you."

"Yes, I'll be in and out."

"I'll let you know how things are with the kids."

"I would appreciate that. Good night."

Becca couldn't get rid of her anxiety by cleaning the kitchen, so she headed outside for a quick brisk walk while some strands of daylight were still lingering. On returning, she approached her front door and was puzzled to find the pot of yellow mums over on its side. *Must have been a large animal running through here to manage that.*

The phone was ringing as she entered the living room. She answered with some trepidation, not sure if she wanted it to be Jack or not.

"Becca, I didn't like the way we left things. I am glad I came home. I've talked with both kids and tried to explain that I know it hasn't been easy being the coach's son—daughter too, for that matter. I want Michael to know that I always watched the other guys and not him because I could count on him to do well, very well. And I know I never praised him, because I didn't want the other kids to have any reason to pick on him. He said he understood. I hope so. Thanks for pointing me in the right direction and sending me home. I hope you and I are still okay. Are we?"

"Thank you for calling. This helps me feel much better about it all. I look forward to seeing you again."

"Me too."

29

The next morning, Becca was sleeping in a bit when she realized someone was knocking repeatedly on the door. She quickly pulled on the jeans and sweatshirt she kept near the bed for just such emergencies, as her habit was to sleep in the nude.

"It's Detective Hawkins, Ms. Collins. Please open up. We have some questions for you."

Still half-asleep, Becca opened the door. "What is so important that you have come all the way to my house at this hour of the morning?" she asked.

"We wanted to catch you before you went to work and disappeared in the migrant camps. There is just one small matter that we need to clear up. It will only take a moment of your time."

Detective Hawkins was painfully aware of the tousled, fresh beauty of the woman who stood there barefoot with no makeup on. He also had the disturbing thought that she had no bra on under that sweatshirt that did nothing to disguise her lovely firm breasts.

"Please come in and sit down. What is this 'small matter'?" she asked them.

"Could you please account again for your time leading up to your visit to LSW on Tuesday night, September 18?"

"As I told you that other morning, Lyons is about forty-five minutes from my home base. My appointment was for eight o'clock. I had had a camp visit at six in Sodus, just off Route 88, Mr. Lawson's camp. There are a number of people who can attest to my presence there. I indulged in a hamburger at Orbaker's on Route 104. Didn't see anyone I knew there. That would have been close to seven till about seven fifteen. Then I headed for my appointment. Got there a couple of minutes late."

"If you had been early, you may have gotten hurt yourself," Detective Hawkins replied. "But do you go to Orbaker's often? Do you know any of the staff who might remember you eating there that particular night?"

"I do tip pretty well. There are a couple of kids that appear to recognize me when I come for a hamburger. I think I even remember one young woman's name, Suzie. And she was there Tuesday night. I think it's a long shot, though, that she would be able to remember my presence that particular night. They were pretty busy."

"Well, even if it is a long one, it's still a shot, and we will follow it up. We need to eliminate everyone we can to get closer to the actual killer. We appreciate your help this morning."

"Oh—maybe I shouldn't have spoken to you without my attorney present," Becca said. She was becoming more and more awake and alert as they conversed.

"I think you'll be very glad you shared this information with us today. We'll get right on it. You can let your attorney know we had this conversation. We'll get back to you after we locate this Suzie. What does she look like, and about how old is she?"

"We've talked, and she told me she's a senior at Riverside High. She's a little shorter than I am and has dark hair pulled back in a ponytail. A very pretty girl."

"Is there anyone else there who would know her or you?"

"Yes, there's Paul, a very tall, blond, surfer-type dude who seems to be around her all the time. And he and I have been friendly."

"Great. Do you know if they start work early or show up close to lunchtime? What time does Orbaker's open each day?"

"I found out one hungry morning that they open at ten. My guess is the kids show up around then to get ready for the lunch crowd."

"One last thing—are you familiar with the Starlight Motel?" Detective Hawkins asked casually.

"Yes, I am. That's where some farmworkers have taken up temporary residence while trying to put down roots here in the North. I've been there several times to visit them," Becca answered easily.

"Have you ever been there with Golden Smith?" the detective sharply asked her.

"No, I have not," Becca answered almost amusedly, reminded of television's Columbo's ploy of leaving the most important question till the end.

"That's it, then," Detective Hawkins pronounced to his partner, and they headed to the door. "Please continue to stay where we can contact you. And if you think of anything else from that night or that might have a bearing on the case, please let us know. You have my card, right?"

"Right," answered Becca as she closed and locked the door behind the police officers.

30

*A*s long as I'm up, I may as well stay that way and get over to the office. Maybe get a little paperwork out of the way before Brick shows up, Becca mused. She decided to upgrade her jeans to black slacks and a soft sea-foam green sweater that was one of her favorites. She made sure Rusty Nail's dishes were full of fresh water and food and headed out.

Becca was impressed to spot Josie's car already in the parking lot as she pulled in. No sign of the press or police, thank God. Their home visit had been more than a little unnerving. Yet, she had high hopes that Suzie or Paul could back up her alibi and confirm that she had spent those important moments miles away from the scene of the murder.

Only Josie and one other employee, Bill, were at their desks as Becca walked in. Josie jumped up and hurried over to

Becca, giving her a warm hug. "You look lovely today," Josie commented. "Not like someone who's been going through the hell you're dealing with."

"Thanks. I feel so supported by you and by my friend Jack, the coach. It's all manageable—at least, it is so far. I keep thinking of how Golden's children and his wife, Noreen, are doing. The funeral is tomorrow, and I'll be sure to be there. Would you prefer holding down the fort here or coming with me?"

"If Brick has gone back, I'd like to go with you. Or do you think he'll be attending it too?" Josie asked.

"Here comes the person in question now," Becca replied as Brick strode in the office door.

"Good morning, gorgeous ladies! Let's grab a cup of coffee, or tea for you, Becca, and head to the conference room to confer for a bit. Unless you've set up a meeting that I don't know about yet for this early hour. Are we free for a while?"

"Yes, we are. I want to report in on yesterday's visits with Reverend Turner and find out your plans for today and tomorrow. Also, I should bring y'all up to date on me and the police."

"Has something more happened?" Josie asked anxiously.

"Yes, I had two early morning visitors, totally unexpected."

"How early morning?" Brick asked. "You're not exactly at your best first thing in the morning," he remarked, chuckling.

"Don't go sounding like you have firsthand knowledge, please. Josie may not have made her mind up about me yet; you don't want to give her the wrong impression of me. I'm just a little slower to get with the program when I first get up. I'd say by after lunch, I'm fine—my usual sharp self."

"After lunch sounds about right," Brick teased. "I try to time my calls for the afternoon when I can."

"Oh, Brick, you don't really do that, do you?" Becca asked with a catch in her voice.

Brick hadn't realized until that moment how close to the edge Becca was feeling. He came around the table and gave her a strong hug. Becca felt tears come to her eyes at this unexpected display of affectionate support.

"Your afternoons and evenings are worth a hundred of another person's mornings!" Brick consoled her. "Now let's get this show on the road and compare some notes on what went down yesterday with the Reverend Joe Turner."

Brick had definitely decided to attend Golden's funeral. "If you can pick me up tomorrow, Becca; I'll turn the state car back in tonight. They have a run on those cars this week. The funeral begins at ten. Would nine thirty work for you?"

"Of course; that will be easy. Will Cliff and John be coming out from Rochester?"

"Since this is our busy season, they're thinking they'll let me do the representing—along with you two, of course. I don't think that's a good call. I told them so, and they said they would hash it out on the way back today. We'll get a call later with the final plan."

"Good. I'm glad you upheld the farmworkers' end of this. I know they walk a fine line with the growers, but we don't want to look like we are downplaying this tragedy. Golden meant a lot to the migrants and farmworkers and to our program also. What do you think, Josie?"

"I only know that his murder has made the national news. I saw a segment on NBC this morning when I was getting dressed, so I'm glad a lot of thought is going into this decision. It's good that you spoke up, Brick—thank you for that."

"You're very welcome. Glad to see you've taken ownership of our little program already. Now, let's see how your numbers stack up against the other two-thirds of the state."

Becca was happy to dwell on a subject that was solid ground for her. Their numbers of migrants and seasonal farmworkers reached and presented with pamphlets exceeded those of the western and eastern sectors. Proportionately, though, the east had more year-round job placements than her team. Becca had two possibilities ahead for next week. She needed to put this murder behind her and concentrate on job development once more. Josie would be a help.

Brick praised them for their efforts so far, generously including Josie in his compliments, and he encouraged them to pick up the pace as soon as they could. "How's that CB contraption working out when you are away from home base?" he asked Becca.

"It's a pretty good connection," she answered.

"I've heard of those," Josie said. "What's your handle—I think that's what they call it?"

"My handle is Southern Comfort," Becca replied. "You'll have to think about getting one too, Josie, so we can talk to each other out in the field."

"I'll look into it this weekend. Are they very expensive?" she asked.

"Not as much as I thought they would be. Maybe we could ask the State for reimbursement. How does that sound to you, Brick?"

Brick laughed. "I'll run it by Cliff, but I wouldn't count on it if I were you two—although now might be a good time to ask for favors. A lot of attention is focused on our little group right now."

"For all the wrong reasons," Becca said with sadness. "New subject. Josie, did you get a chance to order flowers from us for Golden?"

"Yes, they were delivered today and will be at the church tomorrow. Lilies, I believe."

"Lovely."

31

The next morning, Becca debated what to wear to Golden's funeral with limited input from Rusty Nail. She finally chose her tailored gray wool slacks topped by a soft pink sweater.

Brick looked her over appreciatively when she picked him up at his motel. "If I weren't a happily married man, you'd be filing those so-called sexual harassment charges against me morning, noon, and night!"

"That wouldn't be good for our clients." Becca laughed at his backhanded compliment. She was grateful for their easygoing work relationship and for Brick's somewhat awkward attempt at lightening their mood. But she couldn't quite shake her sadness when she thought of what lay ahead for Noreen and the children.

They arrived at the funeral home early, but the main parking lot was already full to overflowing. Becca tried a side street and then another. On the third street over, she found a spot for her Colt and maneuvered her way to the curb.

"Good job," Brick commented as he unfolded his large frame from the Colt's front seat. "I hope Josie is one of those already here."

"I think I spotted her near the entrance when we drove by," Becca replied as they made their way down the intervening street blocks. "I'm curious about who else will be here."

"Let's find Cliff and John and Josie and sit together as a united front," Brick instructed.

Becca spotted Detective Hawkins and his partner hanging back in the crowd that was moving into the church proper. Noreen, Golden's wife, had chosen the local Catholic church, Saint Peter's, for the funeral service.

"There are Cliff and John looking uncomfortable over by the front door. And I do see Josie making her way toward us against the crowd." Becca waved at the two men, who gave a halfhearted acknowledgment back.

Josie was averting her head as she progressed toward them, and it struck Becca how difficult it must be for Josie to confront crowds with her scarred face. Those on this solemn occasion took a quick second look and turned away.

"We're here. Let's get this over with," Cliff grumbled as he joined them.

"We appreciate your coming," Becca said. "I know Golden's wife and family will appreciate it too."

"Let's just keep a step ahead of those photographers."

"We'll do our best and can start by heading on in," Brick replied, steering Becca and Josie toward the front doors.

As they entered, Becca was struck by the peaceful beauty enveloping them. Along each side of the church were stained glass windows depicting different scenes of Jesus teaching and healing and performing miracles. The sunlight filtered through the colored glass, creating beautiful patterns on the people sitting in the pews and on those finding their way in.

Brick motioned for Becca and Josie to precede him into a pew about a third of the way into the church. It was a pretty good vantage point. Becca made use of the remaining minutes before the service started to look around for familiar faces. She was especially looking for Rose. On the way to get Brick, she had been dismayed to realize that she hadn't checked to be sure Rose had a way to the church today. Becca did spot several workers she had personally placed with Golden. There were a number of civic leaders, some who had been helpful and others just seeking the spotlight.

The front of the church was overflowing with floral arrangements. There was a cross made out of yellow and white mums that instantly caught Becca's eye. She was also drawn to a simple arrangement of deep red roses and softly white lilies.

She wasn't very surprised to see Rev. Joe Turner march down the aisle to the very front row and seat himself with Golden's family. It occurred to her that he might be speaking.

Still no sign of Rose, but she may have slipped in the back, or so Becca was hoping.

The casket was solemnly brought down the aisle and carefully placed in front of the altar. One woman near the front started sobbing quite loudly. An elderly gentleman tried to console her with pats on her shoulder and the offer of a handkerchief. She didn't respond to his kindnesses. Then a priest stood up to start the service, having to speak over the still distraught woman.

Becca didn't know her but did recognize Noreen's sister. She assumed the dignified lady to her right was the mother whose arrival had been spoken of when Becca visited the family. Noreen looked lovely in a tailored black suit. The children were in their Sunday best, subdued and a little puzzled by all the pomp and circumstance.

Cliff and John seemed to be having some trouble following the liturgy. Becca felt right at home, having spent many Sundays of her adult life in Episcopal churches.

The priest announced, "We are blessed to have the Reverend Joe Turner here to honor our beloved friend, Golden. Rev. Turner would like to say a few words."

Rev. Turner stood and was silent for a moment. "I must admit that I did not have the pleasure and honor of having been a close personal friend of Golden Smith. However, our lives crossed a number of times as we carried out our mission, working for the betterment of our fellow man and woman. Golden saw the mission in very specific terms and made real his vision of a business, a factory where people could receive an honest day's pay for an honest day's work and be proud of the product they produced.

"He was a husband and a father and a brother. He was taken from his loved ones much too soon. We must see that whoever did this dastardly deed, ending the life of this courageous man, will be caught and punished to the full extent of the law. I personally pledge to each of you here that I will not rest until the coward who committed this monstrous murder is brought to justice."

The church erupted into thunderous applause and many shouts of "Amen!" and "That's right!"

The priest still needed to offer Communion to his congregation and began that process as the crowd settled back down.

Becca didn't know how she felt about Rev. Turner's comments. He had sort of hijacked the service, but he may have brought some comfort to the family and friends in attendance. She could easily guess how her Department of Labor associates were feeling from their body language and Cliff's complaining under his breath to John. Brick looked as nonchalant as ever. Josie looked disturbed and about as sad as Becca was feeling.

Becca joined the line to receive Communion, as it was something she valued. She felt she was more spiritual than religious but still felt that taking Communion was an experience that held meaning for her. As no announcement was made restricting participation, she hoped this was one of the more modern-thinking Catholic churches that welcomed all to the Communion table.

At last, it was all over. The family left the church first with Rev. Turner holding Noreen's arm as they walked down the aisle to the outer doors opened to the crisp fall day.

Becca kept an eye out for Rose as they silently filed out. No sign of her. *I'll be able to stop by her place tomorrow*, she promised herself.

"What's the next step?" asked Josie.

I knew that do-gooder would be here. Too many people around her to smash that pretty head in. He faded into the crowd and did not make eye contact with her, as she did know him a little bit. He would take good care of her. *Maybe tonight.*

Becca felt a prickling at the back of her neck and put it down to the fall breeze. Plus, her sense of foreboding was probably due to the sadness of the occasion. "We can stop by Noreen's home just for a moment. I don't know how her house will hold all these people," Becca said to the group in general.

"We're heading back to Rochester," Cliff announced. "Unless you want to grab a bite to eat first, Brick?" He noticeably left Becca and Josie out of his invitation.

"Yes," said Brick. "We'll let the girls pay our respects to the family, and we'll head back to Rochester. Is that okay with you, Becca and Josie?"

"Of course," Becca replied. What else could she say?

"That's fine with me," Josie chimed in. "I'll follow you over, Becca."

"Maybe it would be better if you ride with me, and I'll bring you back here. One less car to park."

"Good idea. My car's all locked up and can wait in the parking lot for me. Let's go find yours."

As Becca started the Colt, "Fooled Around and Fell in Love" by Elvin Bishop was playing on the radio. She thought about sharing her mixed feelings about the coach with Josie and then decided today might not be the right day for that particular topic. "Josie, tell me about yourself. How are things going so far for you on our job?"

"I really enjoy getting up each day and being around people again. It's been especially good to get to know you—even with all your troubles."

"That's saying a mouthful," Becca replied. "I've really appreciated your steady presence through all this turmoil. Not a great way for you to start a new job. I can promise that we usually have a lot less drama around here, although each day can be different. It does stay interesting. And the people you meet keep you coming back for more."

"I've noticed that already. And I like Brick with all his testosterone on display. Not that sure yet about Cliff. He seems pretty old-school."

"Yes, this group has been a bastion of the old boys' club. We're pretty much seen as the interlopers and do-gooders. Not to mention that we have no business messing in such a traditionally male-dominated business as farming, as well as trying to upset the applecart by offering the migrants and seasonal farmworkers options. I'm optimistic about landing some decent-paying jobs at Miller's next week. I heard they will be hiring. I haven't gotten an appointment yet, as that department hasn't been in place, but I'd like to just drive over on Tuesday—give them Monday to settle in—and take my chances. What do you think?"

"Where you lead, I will follow," Josie answered.

32

They pulled up at Golden and Noreen's home and saw what Becca had anticipated, a street full of cars and trucks. Becca drove around the block and maneuvered the Colt into a tight space between two driveways. She spotted the black Ford Crown Victoria police vehicle belonging to Detective Hawkins and pointed it out to Josie.

"I can't believe there's still a vicious murderer wandering around, maybe even in this very neighborhood right now!" Josie exclaimed.

"Well, we know for sure that the police are well represented at this gathering, so we don't have to worry about our safety right this minute. Let's go pay our respects and then get back to the office—or home, even. I'm hoping to see my friend the coach tonight—or at least talk to him."

"Home sounds good to me today," Josie replied. "I have a dog named Ozzie who has been puzzled by my new schedule of being away from home for long stretches at a time all of a sudden. He's a rescue dog, and it's taken a while to get him to trust me. Getting home before dark tonight would be a big plus for our relationship."

"Home it will be," Becca stated firmly.

They entered the lovely colonial home, making their way through a knot of well-wishers. Golden's children, Becca was happy to see, were chasing two other little ones around the dining room table where a feast had been laid out for the visitors. Platters of ham, fried chicken, and cold cuts vied with humongous bowls of potato salad and coleslaw and two tins of bubbling macaroni and cheese. Deviled eggs were plentiful. Becca could see through into the kitchen where pineapple upside-down cake, a seven-layer chocolate cake, and three of what she guessed were sweet potato pies awaited their turn. She was embarrassed at her excitement over the thought of partaking of these culinary delights.

Josie seemed to be having the same reaction. "I wonder when the eating begins."

Just then, Noreen walked over to the table and started speaking. "I want to thank everyone for coming today and for all your kindnesses. Golden would have been so pleased at this gathering of his friends and family. The ladies of the church outdid themselves on this feast you see before us. Please help yourself to this wonderful food, and thank you again for all your thoughtfulness."

She made her way over to where Becca and Josie were standing and greeted them warmly. Then she slipped out of the room for a moment, hugging each of the children on her way by.

People quickly formed a line for the food. Becca was still looking around for Rose. Detective Hawkins nodded when he caught her eye. Rev. Turner was surrounded by admirers, but he too gave Becca a friendly wave.

There had been a respectful quiet when Noreen addressed the room, but now the level of talk and laughter ratcheted up a few notches. Becca and Josie loaded their plates and picked a window seat to settle down in. Several of Becca's past clients stopped by to say hello and commiserate on how much Golden would be missed.

Soon the desserts were brought out, and Becca was delighted to find that she was right—the pies were sweet potato and not ordinary old pumpkin. She got herself a piece plus a spoonful of banana pudding, loaded with vanilla wafers and bananas.

"Would you call this Southern food or soul food?" Josie asked.

"Both sides get credit. It's Southern soul food or soulful Southern food—take your pick. Either way, it's my favorite."

"Soon to be mine too. Did you grow up eating this way? And how did you get such a beautiful figure with all this as your base?"

"Thank you for that compliment. As you can see, I'm a little extra curvy, because food is such an important part of my life. Good genes help me, I guess. My mother is a petite Southern belle, and my handsome father was slender due to his diabetes. But on my dad's side, there were lots of aunts, uncles, and cousins growing up, and we celebrated every occasion and just about every Sunday with tables full of good food made from both Southern and German recipes. The best of both worlds. I've tried to duplicate my Aunt Nora's crumb cake and my mother's peach-cream pie with graham cracker crust but haven't quite gotten there yet. How about you?"

"My food credentials are 100 percent Italian, and my specialties are biscotti and canolis along with half a dozen other delicious cookies. Wish my calories would distribute themselves in the lovely way yours have. Maybe they'll pick up some pointers if I hang around with you enough."

"Oh, your calories have got the right idea—nothing to be learned from me or mine," Becca said, laughing. Then she collected herself as she looked around at the other participants of this affair.

The children were now settled down with plates of food on their laps and napkins tucked in their necklines in attempts to protect those Sunday outfits. Noreen's mother was chatting with the elderly gentleman whose kindness Becca had made note of at the church service. The woman who had been so distraught was not to be seen among the gatherers.

"Unless you would like a second helping, I think we have done our duty here. What do you think?"

"I think this was an unexpected pleasure that I won't soon forget. Let's find one of those wonderful church ladies and do our best to convey our thanks and sincere appreciation."

"Great idea. The lady in the black hat with red roses was directing the traffic between the kitchen and the tables out here. Let's try her first."

Becca and Josie soon were thanking Miss Ida Jones for the magnificent spread they had enjoyed so much. Then they were on their way to their respective cars and homes—Josie to her dog, Ozzie, and Becca to the hope of hearing from Jack and to the loving presence of Rusty Nail, of course.

I'll just have one more drink, and then it will be dark enough for me to head out to that little house in that apple orchard and give that lousy looking-down-her-nose-at-me bitch what she deserves. I passed right by her in that snooty church, and she didn't even know how close she was to death—her death—and I won't try to make it an easy one! Haven't let the family know I'm here yet. There's time for that. I'll let Miss Goody Two-shoes know how important I am. She'll be begging me to stop or maybe begging me for more—who knows!

33

Becca was so happy to get home to her welcoming house and the warm greetings from Rusty Nail, who was enthusiastically rubbing her ankles and barely letting her make her way in past the front door. Becca glanced through her mail. Nothing too earth-shattering: three charity requests, an electric bill, and a Montgomery Ward flyer.

Not much supper needed tonight, she mused. Mostly she was wondering whether it would be considered too aggressive on her part if she placed a call to the coach rather than waiting for him to call her. She felt he was pretty traditional when it came to male/female dynamics. Yet, he didn't seem at all fazed by the controversy swirling around her with the murder investigation. He might be hesitant to get back in touch with her after their troubling exchanges about his children.

Then the phone rang. She quickly answered on the second ring. It was the man in question. Anticipation danced up and down her whole being. "Is this Becca Collins the Great?" he asked.

"It is, and you have her full, undivided attention."

"Well, I'm afraid I have some bad news—at least, I think it's bad news. I was hoping to come see you tonight, but I can't. My daughter actually wants to spend time with me, and I can't pass that up right now. She wants us to do dinner and a movie. I think it's 'cause the movie *Carrie* would require an adult to get the tickets, and that's where I come in. But I'm looking forward to some one-on-one time with Marcie, especially after my misstep with both of them. Michael has a friend he wants to hang with. Just sorry I can't be in two places at once."

"You need to clone yourself to take care of all your women," Becca teased, hoping it didn't sound as forced to him as it felt to her.

"Oh, right, all my women, all seventy-six of them."

"I'm lucky you can fit me in at all. How was your day up till now?"

"Well, it was pretty usual. Practice went well, and I had a funny thing happen with my 'staff.'"

"What was that?" Becca asked him, wanting to lengthen their conversation as much as she could.

"I've told you about the two kids I call my staff, who are slower than the other kids and get teased a lot. They like to tell their teachers, 'The coach needs me. Gotta do a job for the coach.' And the teachers let them leave the class and come down to me. Today, I didn't have a damn thing for them to do, so I said, 'Sit right there a minute. I'll be right back.' And I slipped down to the equipment room and pulled some uniforms off their hangers and just generally messed the place up a bit. Went back and gave them the keys—they really feel important with those keys—and said, 'Take a look at the equipment room. I'm not sure how it was left last night.' Well, they came back and said, 'Coach, you won't believe how messed up that room is! But we can make it right. Leave it to us.' Before I could turn myself around, they were back in my office telling me to come look at their handiwork. They had made everything spick-and-span in less time than it's taken me to tell you about it. I'm serious! If those kids were in charge of the upkeep of the school, we would sparkle in a jiffy. They are something else." Jack laughed.

Becca laughed with him. She wished they were in the same room so she could reach out and touch him. Hearing his warm, animated voice was almost as good, and they seemed to be back at ease with each other.

"I'd better run get ready for my big night."

"Please tell Marcie hello for me. I'd love to meet her sometime."

"Well, to tell you the truth, I think she has been a little jealous of the time I've been spending with you. She was very close to her mother. Both kids were. Their mom raised them while I did my sports, so the little time I have around my games, I want to be sure to be with them when they'll have me—not like my goof-up last night. But I do want you to meet both of them. Michael will be home again over the Thanksgiving holiday. Maybe you could stop by then. Nothing formal like the actual meal—just drop in for a cup of tea. What do you think?"

"I completely understand their mixed feelings about another woman showing up in your life. I lost my dad at thirteen and was not at all open to my mother's second husband four years later. We can take it slowly and play it by ear. I'm pretty much available that whole weekend, so you just give me a call when you see a good opportunity for me to stop by—or not, if it works out that way."

"Thanks for being so flexible and understanding. You're a good woman. And it must have been really tough to lose your dad so young. Marcy was only eleven, and Michael was the age you were, thirteen, when Lois died. We're making it as a team, and I'm a little scared about doing anything to upset the balance. But I have to tell you, knowing you has greatly improved my life and given me a new and wonderful reason to get up in the mornings. I know we've only known each other a couple of months, but I feel I have found such a good, dear friend in you. Thank you for that."

So many emotions were rolling through Becca's mind and body, the overwhelming one being that of thankfulness— thankful that Jack felt so close to her and appreciated her place in his life; thankful that she had this precious place; thankful that he felt he could share such feelings with her, and so very thankful that the feelings she had for him were reciprocated in kind.

Then there were the fears fighting to take over first place. Fear that she was misunderstanding his interest in her. Fear that she wouldn't be able to relax and simply enjoy his presence in her life. A big fear that his recent insensitivity to his children would show up in his relationship with her.

She didn't know what to say. She was still shaken by his treatment of Michael, though he did smooth it over when he called last night. His words to Michael helped explain his actions for her. Her turn to share. Could she risk letting him know how important he was to her?

"I want to thank you for so many things. Your sharing and openness touch me deeply. And I am so grateful that I am not alone on this journey. I just hope you know how much I have appreciated your standing by me during this troubling time and how much I value having you in my corner—how much I value you, period. I am in awe of your creative mind and your compassionate heart. Now go take your lucky daughter out to dinner. We'll have our time soon."

"Yes, we will. That's a promise!"

With the happy thought that their connection was back reverberating in her brain, Becca relinquished the phone and concentrated on supper. She would grill the piece of salmon she had picked up on the way home, plus cut up the red pepper and a hunk of the head of cauliflower in the refrigerator and sprinkle the pieces with a little olive oil before popping them in the oven for twenty minutes. So delicious and a great finale to all the calories consumed earlier in the day at Golden and Noreen's. She wondered how that family was getting along after the crowd had gone its way and left them with their grief. She hoped the grandmother and aunt were still with them. They probably were.

After a satisfying evening of mindless TV and flipping through some accumulated magazines, Becca got ready for bed. As was her usual habit, she checked the locks on her front and back doors. She was drifting off to sleep when the sound of breaking glass and muffled curses jolted her awake and completely alert, all senses tingled, her muscles tightened. She had no doubt that someone else was in her home and meant her harm. She fell into the jeans and sweatshirt she kept by the bed. She started to tug at the side table, trying to quickly push it against her door. It put up quite a fight. Her crystal lamp fell to the side and shattered, adding to her distress. Rusty Nail let out a cry. She was sickened at the thought that someone may be hurting her precious cat. She filled with rage and was tormented by the thought that she should go to her cat's defense, but she was too scared to do so. Finally, the heavy table was in place. She dialed 911 as her heart beat so hard she thought it would break through her chest. She gave the 911 operator her address. The operator assured her, "We have a car at Cinelli's, which is only half a mile from your location. Just stay calm, and help will be there soon. Do you have a lock on your bedroom door?"

"No, but I did put a heavy table behind it."

"Drag over anything you can to back it up. The police are on their way now. Please stay on the line with me. Has he come upstairs?"

"Yes, he is at my door now. Throwing himself at my door. He must be a big man. The door is cracking! Oh, but I hear sirens now. Thank you! Thank you!"

"You bitch! What have you done now? There you go fucking things up for me again! Just wait. You'll get what you deserve!"

Becca could hear him retreating down the stairs and out the back as the police car pulled in her driveway, lights blazing and siren wailing.

Becca fell onto her bed. She felt like the room was spinning around her. She made herself jump up to meet the police, her heroes, quickly moving the sturdy table blocking her bedroom door and hurrying down the stairs.

"Are you all right, ma'am?" the first officer asked her.

All she could do was nod.

A second policeman came around from the back and reported, "We must have just missed him. I'll put out an APB, and we'll cordon off the neighborhood. Can you describe him, ma'am? Let's go in the living room and sit down. You look a little shaken, which is understandable."

"Yes, please come in, and we'll go sit down. I need to do just that. No, I didn't get any look at him. I did hear his voice, which I know I've heard somewhere before. I just can't place it."

"I'm sure it's frustrating. I'm Officer McCabe, and my partner is Officer Whitestone. The identity of the voice may pop in your head later. Just give us a call the minute it does. I'll give you my card. Is there anyone you would like to call now to come be with you? Or is there a place you could stay tonight while we evaluate the scene? When we're through, probably by morning, you can get that window fixed and feel safe and secure again in your house."

Becca immediately thought of Jack but didn't want to intrude on his night with Marcie. Then Josie came to mind. "I do have someone I work with who probably wouldn't mind my coming over even at this late hour."

"Good. We'll take a quick statement, and you can call your friend. We'll be glad to give you a ride to her home, if you like."

"That sounds awfully good. Let me call and prepare her."

Becca was so glad to hear Josie's familiar voice telling her, "Of course, come right over! I'll put the outside lights on."

34

As they made the drive over to Canandaigua, Becca realized the extent of the commute Josie made each day, although the police car had an easy ride through the small towns and farmlands at this deserted time of night.

Becca sat forward suddenly and tapped the first officer on the shoulder. "You know, I was just realizing that this might somehow have something to do with another horrible incident in my life this past week. I stumbled across a murder in Lyons Tuesday night—Golden Smith's murder. Do you think there could be any connection?"

"That's certainly a possibility. A murder! And you're just now thinking to mention it?"

"I was so frightened by tonight my brain simply wasn't working."

"That can happen. Do you remember the name of the detective who caught the case?"

"Yes, Detective Hawkins. He was very helpful."

"We'll get in touch with him. This may be a good lead. Good that you thought of it."

"Thank you!" Becca was relieved that the brain freeze from her terror was receding at least a bit.

They pulled into the driveway of a modest two-story home all lit up inside and out. Josie had shared with Becca only last week that she had grown up in this home and recently inherited it from her beloved mother, Sarah.

Josie quickly came to the door to meet them with a big hug for Becca. Becca thanked the two officers for their kindness, and they hurried back to their car after turning down Josie's offer of coffee and cookies.

"I would love a cup of tea if you don't mind staying up a little longer," Becca put forth as they headed into the comfortable-looking, lived-in living room. A roomy, green plaid couch was flanked by two deep, green easy chairs. A glassed-in, three-shelf curio cabinet held various framed photos and little Hummel figurines. A bookcase across the room was overflowing with intriguing books of all shapes and sizes. Under other circumstances, Becca would have been itching to examine them for titles and authors. The room felt just as welcoming as the woman who ushered Becca into its space.

"I was thinking some hot chocolate might help us get to sleep more easily," Josie told her.

"That would be lovely," Becca replied tiredly. "I simply can't believe what happened tonight!"

"Tell me about it, and then we'll lose ourselves in chocolate."

"I was so scared! I kept hearing crashes from downstairs in the kitchen and then his getting closer and closer as he came up the stairs. I just know that I've heard his voice somewhere before, and I can't come up with it yet. Maybe when I meditate or even when I'm falling asleep tonight, the answer will come. And the things he was saying! Who could hate me that much, someone whose voice I can't put a name to? When Rusty Nail cried out, I was petrified! Thank God he's all right."

Josie put her arm around Becca and helped her sit down on the sofa. They heard the pitter-patter of paws, and then a golden-brown being hurled himself up on the sofa between and on top of the two women.

"Ozzie, get down! Don't forget your manners. This is our friend Becca. Becca, this is Ozzie the Great."

"Ozzie, what a love you are!" Becca embraced the warm, wriggling body of the happy dog.

"Let me get our hot chocolate and a treat for Ozzie, and we'll be all set."

Becca was feeling 1,000 percent better than she had before reaching this oasis of safety in her sea of troubles. She was sure nothing bad could happen to them with Ozzie on the alert.

Josie returned holding a tray on which balanced two oversized mugs, steaming and emitting a heavenly fragrance, plus a plate overflowing with homemade biscotti—just right for dipping, Becca was sure.

"Josie, I love your home. It's so warm and welcoming. I couldn't have asked for a better place to come to tonight. I can't thank you enough!"

"You are so very welcome. Ozzie and I love company. I think he gets bored with just me around most days. And he certainly has taken a liking to you."

Ozzie was curled up in a heap at Becca's feet, tail thumping away.

"I know dogs and cats should not have chocolate. Will it be okay with you if I slip him a little bite of one of your other cookies, or is he on a special diet?"

Ozzie looked up expectantly, following this conversation closely.

Josie laughed. "You're so right about chocolate, but beyond that, the sky's the limit where Ozzie's concerned. Right, boy?"

Ozzie's whole body completely agreed with Josie.

"I do sort of keep track of treats to keep his weight under control. But he's so active it really hasn't been a problem."

"Well, I'm going to pretend I'm Ozzie and eat and drink with abandon tonight!" Becca declared, grateful for this switch to ordinary conversation.

"Go for it!"

That night, Becca, tucked under one of Josie's Aunt Angie's hand-crocheted blankets, slept fitfully. But each time she awakened with a start, she was comforted by the gentle snoring of Ozzie, who had taken up a command post at the foot of her bed. No bad guys would get by him!

The next morning, Becca again complimented Josie on her comfortable home. Josie explained, "I am really fortunate to have been given this happy place to live. All I have to worry about are the taxes and the insurance. That's a good thing, as the money gene missed the Lombardi family. Grandpa Lombardi was the only little old Italian bootlegger in New York State who went bankrupt."

On that happy thought, they headed back to Wayne County in Josie's six-year-old Ford Mustang. "Take Five" by Dave Brubeck was playing on Josie's car radio. Becca's spirits soared along with the music. Her mind went out to play with the intricate notes that drew her out of herself and far away from her troubles.

35

"Let's swing by your house and see if the police are through doing their thing. Then you can arrange for a replacement of your window, and when you get home tonight, your house will be all back to itself. Unless you'd like to spend another night at my house. Ozzie and I would love that."

"Thank you, Josie. It's good to go back home in the daytime. I need to get back in my routine and check on Rusty Nail. The police did say they would have a car close by checking in on me, so I'll be fine. If I'm really lucky, Jack could stop by tonight. I'll give him a call and bring him up to date—Brick, too, when we get to the office."

"Good plan."

Her house had a deserted air about it, Becca thought. Of course, what was disconcerting was the yellow crime-scene tape cordoning off the back and side of the cottage. Someone had gone to the trouble of sweeping up the glass in the kitchen. Becca pulled out the yellow pages for Wayne County and soon had an appointment for later that day to have a new window installed in her home. Rusty Nail came out of hiding to greet her and Josie with much ankle rubbing.

"I hope he wasn't too worried last night. He's not used to spending the night alone. And then the police technicians! An interesting twenty-four hours—right, Rusty Nail?"

Rusty Nail was pointedly over by his food dishes. Becca had given him fresh water before she left the night before, but it was time to replenish the hard stuff. Priorities.

"Well, I think we're all set here. Let's head to Sodus and see how things are going on that front."

"Do you need to check back with the police? Oh, there's a car with two serious-looking men in it pulling in your driveway now."

The doorbell rang, and Becca was surprised to see Detective Hawkins and his pleasantly ugly sidekick on her doorstep.

"I noticed on the police log that you had an uninvited visitor last night. Do you mind if we come in, and you can fill us in on what happened?"

"Come in, of course. Are you thinking there's a connection between my break-in and Golden's murder?"

"Let's put our heads together and see if there is a connection."

Becca reintroduced Josie and explained that they were on their way to work.

"This shouldn't take too long. The report I read stated that you felt the perpetrator's voice was familiar. Have you been able to connect a name or face to that voice?"

"No, it's just out of reach. Usually when I meditate, answers to problems or reminders of tasks to do will pop in my head. But so far, I've had no luck with putting together this particular puzzle. Really wish I could come up with it!"

"Well, I'm sorry you had this scare. Would you mind running through what happened one more time for me and Detective Kaiser?"

"Anything to catch this guy. But all I know is that I had turned off the lights, checked the front and back doors, and had just settled into my bed waiting for Rusty Nail when I heard glass breaking and then a male voice cursing as he started up my stairs." Becca's stomach turned over as she remembered her terror listening to the intruder plow his way up to her bedroom.

"About what time did this occur?"

"Five or ten minutes after eleven. I dragged a heavy table over to the door—it has no lock—and quickly called 911. They should have a record of the time."

"Doesn't this prove that Ms. Collins had nothing to do with Golden's death?" Josie interjected.

"It just might if we get a match on fingerprints from the kitchen and from Golden's office—that are not yours, of course."

Becca felt she was seeing light at the end of her hellish tunnel. Maybe this scary incident would help end the nightmare that continued to envelop her.

"Well, we have a patrol car assigned to your lane through the orchard on a regular basis. It wouldn't hurt to get a lock installed on that bedroom door. We did get a bunch of prints, and once we sort them out, we'll check back with you for further identification. Where will you be the rest of today?'

"I'll be checking in at my home base in Sodus. I do have a client I want to see in Lyons. No other firm plans. Oh, someone is coming to fix the window in the late afternoon, if that's okay, so I'll be here then. I'm feeling a bit frazzled and may stay home tonight instead of making any camp visits."

"Fine. We'll track you down as soon as we come up with our list of people who have been in this home recently. You could make a list also of those you remember being here."

"Good. Thank you for your efforts and for your concern. We didn't even offer y'all any coffee. Would you like some?"

"No, we'll keep pursuing this lead. You ladies have a nice day." The two men headed out the door to their nondescript car.

Josie and Becca piled in the Mustang. "You must have gotten this car right when they first came out. How long did you say you've had it?"

"Six years. I decided to do something really wild with the insurance money from the fire. Something very unlike me. Plus, the car pulls people's attention away from my face and draws it to itself. Especially the first couple of years when it was such a novelty. And it's just a fun car!"

"I'm glad you have it," Becca replied.

36

Soon they were pulling up to the office building where Becca had left her car. Becca knew she had to call Brick and let him know the latest, but every ounce of her body urged her to hop in her car and go to Jack.

I have to call Brick first. Jack is probably involved in a class or meeting this early in the day. I'll wait. I could call him and see if we could meet for lunch. I'll do that, she promised herself as motivation to get herself and her body inside the building.

Lillian, the receptionist, stopped her on the way in and handed her a pink memo slip. Jack had called her, asking if she could share lunchtime with him. She felt light-headed by their connection and at the thought of seeing him in just a couple of hours.

She dialed the school number hoping it would be a direct connection to Jack. It was.

"How was your night with Marcie?"

"It went really well. We even touched on the subject of boys."

"I want to hear more about that!" Becca teased him. Then she got serious and said, "I do have something important to share when we get together. Since your time is more limited than mine, may I swing by and pick you up? Would noon work for you?"

"Perfect. I'll be outside waiting. Let's make it 11:58."

Brick was appropriately appalled by her recounting of the terror of the night before. "I don't want you to be alone in that house until they catch this guy. How soon will they get back to you? Did they put any kind of a rush on the fingerprint info or whatever they do?"

"Well, the detective who is in charge of Golden's investigation has latched onto this incident. That alone makes me feel better. I'll give them a call before I head out to Lyons later this afternoon. First, I have a quick lunch date with my friend, the coach."

"He sounds like quite a guy. Could he camp out at your house till this case is solved?"

"He has his children to consider, and I don't know that we're at the point in our relationship that I could ask him something like that. I'll see how it goes today. I did spend last night with Josie and Ozzie."

"Who's Ozzie? Josie has a boyfriend stashed away that you two haven't told me about?"

"Ozzie is a very handsome, very loving guy who's not afraid to show his emotions. He's also a gorgeous golden retriever. You just have to meet him soon."

"I'll put that high up on my to-do list," Brick promised. "Now is Josie going with you to Lyons?"

"Yes, I think so."

"Well, give me a call after your big lunch date. I want to be sure you have a plan in place for tonight. It would be a lot of trouble to train someone to take your place."

"Don't worry about my doing the job. Although I may skip the camp visits tonight after the sun goes down."

"There's no *may* about it! That's a direct order from me to you. No night camp visits for you or Josie till we get this guy behind bars where he belongs. Are we clear on that?"

"Sure. And, again, there's nothing to worry about. The police are making Gates Drive a regular part of their patrol routine. I'll definitely figure something out for tonight. Maybe it will even be all over by then. I think part of me is glad about last night if it just brings all this to a conclusion."

"Certainly we can hope for that, but in the meantime, let's keep you safe. Keep things running smoothly, requiring little effort on my part. Don't forget to call me."

"I won't forget. Thanks, Brick, for your concern."

"Right, right. Have a good lunch."

Becca relayed the conversation to Josie. "That's the closest he'll get to saying he would miss me if that guy took me out."

"He's a real softie under all that machismo, isn't he?" Josie put forth.

"He's the best!" Becca agreed. "What're your lunch plans, Josie?"

"I'm going to see whether Lillian would like to run up to Orbaker's for one of their scrumptious hamburgers. Then I may try my hand at job development with an old friend of mine in Canandaigua, if that's all right with you."

"How wonderful! Very good luck with it. Can't wait to hear the results."

37

Becca's heart was racing as she pulled into the parking area outside the high school, dismayed to find that it was already 12:02 as she parked the Colt. Jack was at the gate of the fence surrounding the school, tapping at his watch and shaking his head at her technical tardiness.

What caught Becca completely by surprise was the flood of tears that broke forth at the sight of Jack and his supposed disapproval. He hurried over to her car as she fumbled with the door lock on his side of the Colt.

"Are you all right? Would you like to come inside to my office and I'll get you a drink of water? Becca, are you all right?"

He had gotten himself into the car and had one strong arm around her heaving shoulders while wiping away her many tears with his other hand.

Becca was again overcome, this time by embarrassment. She buried her face in his shoulder for a moment to regain her composure and then asked him, "Sorry I'm making a scene here at your place of work."

"Absolutely you are! Everyone within five miles of us is frozen in place, just waiting to see what you'll do next. Please, Becca, can you tell me what's wrong?"

Becca took a deep breath. Then another. "Everything is all right now that I'm with you. Last night, someone broke into my house. I think he really wanted to hurt me. And I was worried he'd hurt Rusty Nail. He came up my stairs. I had barricaded myself in my bedroom. The police were over at Cinelli's, so they got there in time to scare him away. Didn't catch him, though. But Jack, if this is the same guy that killed Golden, I'm off the hook completely. Wouldn't that be wonderful?"

"Of course it would be. But time-out. Let's get back to last night. He didn't actually touch you or get in the same room with you—is that right?"

"That's right. When the sirens started sounding in the distance, he went back down my stairs. I was so grateful. I'll never feel the same way about sirens again."

"I should have been there. I would have beaten him to a pulp, or at least slowed him down a little. Why didn't you call me when all this was going on? I'm serious."

"You were having your night with Marcie, and I didn't want to interrupt that special time. It's probably good that you weren't there. I don't know what might have happened."

"Well, I'd feel a whole lot better if I had my chance with this asshole. You didn't get a look at him?"

"No, I heard his voice saying terrible things, and I really think I've heard that voice somewhere before."

"Well, I'm just damn glad that the bastard didn't touch you or even get near you. And this was his only shot at it. I'll be camping out at your house till he's all locked up."

"Jack, did Michael go back to school? What about Marcie? And what people will think and say?"

"You know me by now—that I don't give a damn what people think or say except when it comes to your reputation. That is something we need to keep in mind. Let me think about this. I could hole up somewhere close by outside, but I wouldn't feel as confident about that. I want to be where I can keep an eye squarely on you at all times. You may not have noticed, but you've become an important part of my life, and I'm not about to let some fool mess that up or mess you up. You can count on it!"

As they were talking, Jack was caressing Becca's arm, and he gave it a squeeze for emphasis. Becca felt her stress melting away and her libido kicking in instead. She so wanted to lose herself in his arms and stay surrounded by his marvelous body till this drama played its last act.

But this was not the time or place. They pulled apart as if on an unspoken count. Jack leaned back in and kissed her cheek chastely.

"Michael is on his way back to Ithaca. Don't you worry about Marcie. She will welcome any excuse to camp out at her friend Janice's house. No arguments. I'll get my gear and be at your house right after practice. Cut it off a little early tonight and definitely be in your home before the sun goes down."

"I'll make you a good supper," Becca promised. "Is there anything you especially like or dislike?"

"I'm your typical meat-and-potatoes guy, but I really like vegetables too. I've had a hankering for lima beans lately, if you are able to hunt some down. But anything you come up with will be great, Becca. We can do a fancy thought-out meal some other time when you have days to plan and prepare. Hot dogs and beans would be perfect tonight if that works for you."

"This talk has gotten me hungry. Let's hit the road and see if we can find an open booth at Friendly's."

Becca was mentally revamping her afternoon plans. The main visit she wanted to make was to Lyons to check in on Rose, and she wanted to get the Spanish translation brochure of the new health center over to the Gonzales family. The mother had had complications after the stillbirth of their fourth child, a little girl. After that, she could do a little grocery shopping for tonight's special dinner guest. The thoughts of what could transpire after dinner were dancing around in her brain and tying her stomach into knots. Would she finally be able to let her guard down? She wondered if all the trust she felt for Jack would allow her to be at ease in his presence and be receptive to any physical connections they might make.

They had been taking it slowly, and she wasn't sure whether it was by choice or just because of all of life's interruptions. Tonight might bring answers, maybe earth-shattering ones.

38

Becca knew Rose worked the 7:00–3:00 shift, so she should be home at 3:30. As she pulled up to the gray, weather-beaten house on this run-down street, Becca could see the yellow school bus turning the corner two blocks away, having dropped off its precious cargo.

Danny, Rose's eldest, answered the door to their apartment and then disappeared, leaving Becca alone with little Nettie Mae.

"My daddy hit my momma hard," Nettie Mae said. "He hurt her."

"I know, sweet baby. But we don't let that happen anymore now," Becca consoled the four-year-old, remembering the sad way they had met a few months before. Becca had shown up just after a fight between the parents that was very one-sided. She had encouraged Rose to get advice from the battered women's shelter in Williamson.

"Nettie Mae, you go play with your doll baby now." Rose had quietly entered the room. Even the heavy makeup couldn't hide the fresh bruise running along her left cheekbone.

Becca felt like she had been hit by a bolt of lightning. "Was Otis here? Was he here last Tuesday night?"

"Please, I don't want any more trouble. Please, Miz Becca. I just slipped and fell. That's all. Nothin' to worry about."

"Rose, you have to tell me. Was Otis anywhere near Wayne County Tuesday night?"

"Don't you no never mind, Miz Becca. Otis, he got nothin' to do with all this."

"Rose, someone broke into my home last night, and now I'm thinking the voice I heard coming up my stairs may have been Otis's. I thought he was in Florida, but you just have to tell me if he was in New York when Golden was killed and if he is still somewhere around here."

Rose broke into sobs, reaching out to Becca to steady herself. Becca quickly put her arm around Rose and led her to the couch.

"Otis, yes, he be here now and last week. When he hit me, it was 'cause he thinks I come on to other men, and it makes him like a wild man. He don't like it one bit that I goes to work where so many men are. But I swear, Miz Becca, I never did nothin' to encourage those men, especially not Mr. Smith. But Otis, he just don't believe me." Rose pulled herself together somewhat. "You'd best leave, Miz Becca. We'll talk another day. I 'preciate all you've done for us, but we don't need nothin' more right now. Okay? Just leave now before trouble comes."

"Is that a pay phone out in the hall? I really need to use it."

"Please just go, Miz Becca!"

"I'll go, but I'll be back. Will you and your children be okay till I get back?"

"Yes, we be fine. You just go now. Quick."

"Would you three come with me? Is Otis still in town? Where is he right now?"

"We're just fine right here, Miz Becca. Otis is out looking for work. We'll see him come suppertime." Rose was practically pushing Becca out her door when it burst open.

"Woman, what are you doing in my home? I want you out of my life—permanently! And I can see to that right now."

Becca was terrified while not understanding why this man held such animosity toward her. "Otis, I will certainly leave your home. But why do you hate me so?"

"Bitch, you've taken everything from me. Getting my woman to go to that factory wasn't enough for you. Oh no. You, a stupid, snobby white woman, got picked over me for that Department of Labor job! I'm the one with MSFW experience—you don't know shit about it! They hustled me out of there just 'cause I had a drink or two in me. Wanted a lily-pure white woman. Makes no sense! But I'll get you erased from this wrong picture. Then they'll be glad to have me work for them. And Rose can stay home where she belongs!"

Otis lunged across the room toward Becca where she was cornered in their tiny apartment.

But Nettie Mae came running into the room and said, "Daddy, this be Miss Becca, my friend." She threw her little self at his right leg and held on determinedly, as he stumbled over her little body.

Becca took this opportunity to slide toward the door. Then she was out in the hallway. "I'll be back in a little while. Danny, you stay with your mother, all right?" she yelled through the closed door.

Becca felt torn between making sure Rose and Nettie Mae and Danny were safe and the need to get this vital information to Detective Hawkins as quickly as possible. She knew now that the voice she had heard in her home was that of Otis. Golden had mentioned that he wanted to discuss something concerning Rose. Could he have been involved with her and Otis found out about it—and beat him to death?

She heard Otis come through his door right behind her. She ran out in the street to her car, hopped in, and drove toward the part of town that would have some kind of a store or restaurant with a pay phone. She spotted the Lyons Police Department beside the county courthouse, a welcome sight.

Becca ran inside, frantic, asking the sergeant on duty at the information station, "Please, can you find Detective Hawkins for me as quickly as possible? Please hurry. It's urgent!" She thought this might be his home base and was very much in hopes that he would be nearby.

He strode into the reception area and greeted her with surprise. "Ms. Collins, do you have something to tell me that will help us with the Golden Smith case? We're getting nowhere with the fingerprints we lifted from your home."

"Detective, I'm almost certain I know whose voice I heard last night. And he is right here in Lyons. He just threatened to kill me!"

"Do you need medical attention? If not, let's head for one of our conference rooms, and you can give me a statement on what has happened. Let's start with an address where we can find this perp if you have it for us. We'll get a car over there right now. We'll take care of it; don't you worry."

Becca gave him the address before the detective hurried away to make the arrangements. "Please be very careful, as there are two children in the apartment along with my client Rose Washington. Danny, her son, is about sixteen but could be mistaken for an adult. His little sister, Nettie Mae, is only four. They live in the first-floor apartment on the left as you enter the building."

"Thanks, Ms. Collins. I think it would be good if you head back to your home and let us contact you there later when we have apprehended the suspect. We'll keep a car there in case he tries to go back to your home again."

"Since people are worried about me right now after last night, it probably is good that I head for home. Please do let me know what happens."

"Will do. I'll walk you partway out."

Becca wondered if she should go back to Rose's apartment and scoop her and the children up to keep them out of danger. But the police work was already in motion, and she knew she mustn't get in the way. She would head straight home and wait patiently by her phone for Detective Hawkins to give her the good word. No stopping by the store to get tonight's dinner fixings. She would play the next few hours by ear. She knew Jack would understand.

She rushed to her car and pointed it west, back to Rusty Nail and Jack and whatever the night would hold.

39

Sitting in her driveway was Jack's 1972 medium-blue Chevy Impala. Jack quickly approached her Colt between raindrops and opened the car door for her. "I've been thinking about you ever since you left the school parking lot. How are you?"

"I'm fine. I have something big to tell you. Let's get inside out of all this rain and wetness."

Rusty Nail greeted them warmly with many ankle rubs and loud purrs and seemed happy to see the coach again.

"I've brought my gear, and Marcie is quite glad to spend the night with Janice."

"That's great, but you may not need to stay. I think we've figured out who the killer is, and I'm quite positive I know who was in my house last night."

"Okay. All right, then. Who is it? I'll go tear him a new one for scaring you like he did."

"You know Danny Washington, of course. And you met Rose, his mother. She has an on-again, off-again boyfriend named Otis Brown. I thought he was in Florida looking for work, but he has been up here in Wayne County. He has been violent with Rose in the past—very possessive of her. If he thought there was anything going on between Rose and Golden, that might explain Golden's beating death. Otis just threatened to kill me! He thinks my job of outreach worker should have gone to him, but he said he showed up drunk for his interview, so I guess they had no choice to not hire him."

"Whoa. Slow down a minute. Did he hurt you? Where did you see him? Did you go to the police?"

"The police are going to pick him up and interrogate him. They're at his house right now, but I don't know if he's home or not. I told the police that Rose, Nettie Mae, and Danny were in the apartment. I should have scooped them up, but I thought I should stay out of the way of the police for now. They will call and let me know when they get Otis. At the least, they could put him in jail for breaking into my house. And what in the world are you doing here on a late afternoon? A little rain wouldn't stop you and your team from practicing, right?"

"Right. They're still at it. I asked Coach Sweet, my second in command, to take over. We've already concentrated on stopping the passing game that Friday night's team is known for. If they get to leave a little early today, they're good kids. They deserve it. Have you checked your answering machine yet?"

"I can see from here that there's nothing on it. Come sit down, and I'll make us a cup of tea."

"I'll make the damn tea. You tell me what happened to you this afternoon. I'm so sorry if Danny's family is mixed up in all this mess," he continued. "He's been busting his hump to move up a spot on the team, but he wasn't in school today. He doesn't need all these distractions."

"Rose doesn't need this, either," Becca replied sadly as she headed for the kitchen to help make their tea.

Jack walked into the small kitchen area and came up behind Becca, placing his arms around her waist and squeezing her tightly to his chest, molding her body to his. "I just want to give you a proper hello," he said as he kissed the back of her neck tenderly.

The phone started ringing, and they both jumped away from each other. Becca quickly moved to the living room to answer the intruding instrument.

"Yes, this is Becca Collins. Rose Washington is asking for me? And Detective Hawkins is requesting that I return to Lyons at my earliest convenience? Yes, I can turn around and come back now. May I bring a friend with me? Thank you. Yes, it will be within the hour. Good-bye."

She turned to Jack. "That was a policewoman calling for Detective Hawkins; they have Otis in custody. Jack, can I ask you to go with me? I'll treat you to supper on the way back."

"Of course I'll go with you. I'm yours for the night or as little or as much of it as you want me for."

Becca felt a flush of sexual excitement run through her body at the thoughts of what a whole night with Jack could mean. For now, she must focus on the job at hand. Turning off the teapot, she asked Jack, "Will you be able to make this trip without fortifications?"

Jack reached behind her and grabbed two bananas from her multicolored fruit basket. "This will keep us going." He took her hand and led her out to his car. "I'll do the driving this trip, and you can unwind and fill me in more what happened today."

40

They pulled into the police station parking lot in Lyons as the sun was beginning its descent into the ribbon of darkness on the far horizon.

Becca jumped out of Jack's car, not waiting for his polite opening of the door. He hurried to catch up with her as she pushed ahead toward the glass doors of the imposing police station. Its gray brick facade was a gloomy portent of the grave business conducted inside its walls.

They stopped at the same information desk where there had been a changing of the guard. A new shift brought about another sergeant who looked a lot younger than the one Becca had encountered earlier.

"We're here to see Detective Hawkins."

"One moment, ma'am."

That was all the time it took for Detective Hawkins to materialize in the waiting area. He greeted them perfunctorily and led them back to another nondescript conference room.

"Detective Hawkins, this is Jack Hightower, a good friend of mine. I hope it's all right that he stays with me."

"Couch Hightower, it's a pleasure. I've been on the losing end of your outstanding coaching on the playing field. It's really good to meet you in person. Sorry about the circumstances, though."

"Yes. Please tell us if you have this scumbag in custody."

"Mr. Otis Brown is being held as a person of interest. We need the help of Ms. Collins to determine whether he is our perp or not. Ms. Collins, we'll ask you to participate in a lineup behind a one-way mirror where the men won't be able to see you. It will be dark so you won't see them either. We'll have each of them say a few words to see if they trigger your memory of that night in your home. Do you have any questions for me before we get started?"

"No, that's all pretty straightforward. I do have a question as to where Rose and the children are right now. I believe she asked for me earlier."

"Yes, she did. Our social worker, Ms. Lieberman, took the three of them down the street to the diner. The little one was getting hungry. They'll be back by the time we're through here."

"Sounds like they're in good hands. If it's Mary Ann Lieberman, I worked with her on the battered women project, and she's wonderful."

"Glad you think so. Now, let's get started. If you'll both just follow me, we're going down the hall to the first door on the right."

Becca was so grateful for Jack's calm presence beside her, his hand resting on her forearm as they followed the detective down the hall.

They entered a grim, darkened room, the main feature of which was a long glass partition facing the door through which they had come. On the other side of the glassed wall, five men— three white, two black—were lined up holding numbers in front of their chests. Detective Hawkins ushered Becca and Jack to the two front seats facing the one-way glass window. Becca could barely make out the outlines of the men's bodies in the darkened room. The detective then spoke into a microphone, instructing the men, "Step forward when your number is called and repeat these words: 'You bitch! Just look what you've done now!' Speak clearly. Don't mumble."

As each man repeated the hateful words, Becca gripped the edge of her folding chair, concentrating on remembering that terrifying night, attempting to match the intruder's voice with that of one of the voices being presented to her.

"Number one, step forward. Repeat 'You bitch! Just look what you've done now!'"

The first man sounded amused by the words he was repeating. He didn't sound at all like the voice that was etched in Becca's memory bank.

The second man had a pronounced Jamaican accent—beautiful to hear even around the ugly words he spoke.

Then the third man spoke in a low monotone, but Becca was almost certain it was the same man who had broken into her little home.

She waited until the last two had spoken and then asked, "Would you have number three say the words again?"

"Number three, step forward. Repeat 'You bitch! Just look what you've done now!'"

Number three did so with a little more feeling, possibly angry at being asked to repeat this exercise.

"I am sure. That is the same voice I heard on my stairway two nights ago. I am very sure it is."

Becca was trembling and very grateful Jack had moved close beside her with his arm around her shoulders, steadying them.

Detective Hawkins instructed his colleague, "Let all the men go except number three. Thank you." He turned to Becca. "Let's go back down the hallway and do a little paperwork, Ms. Collins. Are you up to that?"

"Yes, absolutely. Just please tell me—was the man whose voice I identified Otis Brown?"

"Yes, ma'am, that's exactly who it was. We are working right now on tying him to Golden Smith's murder—and, of course, his threats to you earlier today."

"This is almost over." Becca leaned into Jack, almost collapsing as relief washed over her like a tidal wave.

After the paperwork was completed, they were walking down the hallway when Nettie Mae came running toward Becca, followed quickly by her mother and brother and another lovely woman in her fifties. Becca scooped the four-year-old up in her arms and greeted the others. She introduced Jack to the social worker. "Mary Ann, I am so very glad to see you! This is my friend Jack Hightower, who is also Danny's coach."

"So glad to meet you, Coach."

"Likewise."

Jack threw an arm around Danny, placing him in a pretend choke hold. Danny grinned with pleasure.

"Rose, I'm so sorry for the way this has turned out, but I'm very glad you and the children will be safe now. Nettie Mae, thank you so much, sweetheart, for saying I was your friend today to your daddy. It helped me a lot." Becca gave Nettie Mae a kiss.

"I'm the one who's sorry, Miz Becca," Rose replied tearfully.

"Please don't worry," Becca said. "It's all over now. Do you and the kids need a ride home?"

"No, that's all taken care of," Mary Ann said smoothly. "I believe Detective Hawkins wants to have a few more words with Rose while I show Nettie Mae and Danny around the police station. So good to see you, Becca, and to meet you, Coach."

"Good to meet you too and to have your help."

"I'll be looking for you at practice tomorrow, Danny. We need you to give that quarterback a good workout."

"I'll be there, Coach. You can count on me."

"I know I can. You take good care of your mother and your little sister tonight."

"Yes, sir."

"Rose, I'll be out your way late tomorrow afternoon and will stop by, if that's okay," Becca added.

"I'd appreciate it, I would."

Becca hugged Rose and Mary Ann and each of the children. Hard. She and Jack headed for his car. As they pulled out of the parking lot, Becca could hardly believe it was over.

"I so hope Rose doesn't blame herself for all this."

"I liked it that you didn't play down her part in all this mess since we really don't know exactly what happened. Danny's a good person, and I think he'll be there for his mom tonight."

"Can I buy you supper somewhere on our way home?"

"What I want right now, Becca, is just to be in your cozy house holding you in my arms and letting all this sink in and then swirl away from us like water down a drain."

Becca nestled in close to his body as he swiftly secured their homecoming.

41

They walked in her front door, and Jack turned to her, pulling her into his embrace as his lips found hers. That kiss grew in intensity more quickly than Becca could take in what was happening. Suddenly, she was tugging at her sweater, at his shirt, as he was trying to release her from her cumbersome clothing.

There was too much between them, and then there was nothing, nothing keeping them from full enjoyment of each other's bodies.

They clumsily moved as one toward the living room couch. Becca could feel every inch of his body pressing against hers, and all she desired was that Jack be inside her and she be one with this cherished man.

He entered her, filling her need for him and reaching deep inside to her very core, the pure overwhelming love that was there for this man and for this man only.

They merged as one. Whole. Complete. Home free. Touchdown for the home team!